TI

2 C
FROM C
WITH
LOVE

Craig Newnes is a Consultant Critical Psychologist, editor, musician and author. He has published numerous book chapters and academic articles and is editor of *The Journal of Critical Psychology, Counselling and Psychotherapy*. He was, for 19 years, the editor of *Clinical Psychology Forum,* the in-house practice journal of the Division of Clinical Psychology of the British Psychological Society and director of Psychological Therapies for Shropshire's Community and Mental Health Services Trust.

He has edited six books and is commissioning editor for six volumes in the Critical Psychology Division from PCCS Books. His latest books are *Clinical Psychology: A critical examination* (2014) and *Children in Society: Politics, policies and interventions* (2015). *Inscription, Diagnosis, Deception and the Mental Health Industry: How Psy governs us all* (2016) and, with Laura Golding, he edited *Teaching Critical Psychology* (Routledge, 2018). He has been an Honorary Professor at Murdoch University and an Honorary Lecturer at seven UK universities. In 2005, he received the CCHR Award in Human Rights for twenty years of speaking out about the PSY Complex.

With his dad he has written a history of the Malaysian Emergency. Hidden on his computer he has an illustrated children's book, *Finnledoo*. He is a dad and gardener and does his best to be a good Jewish boy.

Tearagh't

A novel

Craig Newnes

THE REAL PRESS
www.therealpress.co.uk

Published in 2017 by the Real Press
www.therealpress.co.uk

ISBN (print) 978-1912119622
ISBN (ebook) 978-1912119615

To my grandmother and my ever tolerant family

Acknowledgements

With thanks to Norman Ackroyd for kind permission to use *Inishtearagh't* as the front cover, Mike Goldmark of the Goldmark Gallery, Uppingham, the generosity of the people of Vigo and, of course, David Boyle.

Contents

I Being the manne's tale 3

II Being the woman's tale 139

III *Coda* – Being the decision 231

Part One

Being the manne’s tale

Thysse message is o'er long. It doth comprise two main parts, a briefe note from one of mie oarsmenne on the findinge of the Spaniartt's papers and the translat'd papers themselffes. These are in onlie part sensible order as the oarsman had yet to right them and the manne that translat'd the Spanish writinge simplye retold the tale in the order receiv'd. The originale paperes have disapper'd thysse xi daie of September 1589. They were soak'd butte legible and found bound at the stern of a small craft adrift in the baie call'd Coumenole.

The baie is rough of sea as are all these parts but once trapp'd by the tide any vessel doth circle against the sands until the tide turns. The water's edge is easily reach'd from the cliffes and mie man hath some strength. He caught the boat, gain'd the papers and sent them for translation that very daie. He has since sent them to me with hysse note attach'd, in case there was newes of Felipe's plans.

I shall give a small sketch of Coumenole and its vista. Off the south west corner of Irellande lie the Blaskete islands. These are home to a small and strangely independent community of families. An Blascoad Mor is the only island with housinge and shelter. Its fresh water allowes islanders to live, raise their families and work within view of the mainland (Coumenole is due North East from the Great Blaskete, about 10 leagues distance) with no need to cross the treacherous sounde in search of sustenance. All around here the spoken tongue is Gael. Ffrench and Spanish are known - An Dingaen is a Spanish resort of sorts.

The island families live by some fishinge, the raising of roote crops and a ceaseless supplye of gull eggs. The occasionale seal pup will find itselffe wash'd upon the strand where it shalle meet a quicke death at the hands of the island children – who knoweth a feast when they see one.

Beyond An Blascoed Mor (the Great Blaskete) lies An Tearacht, a terrible and lonelie rock that stands proud of the waves less than a cable high and perhappes ten across at yts base. Yt cannot be seen from the islanders' homes for they lie to the easterne lee of the Blaskete ridge. From a distance Tearagh't has a pinnacle that might appear the top of the most perfect mountain. From there to the West lies nought but oceane.

The paperes take the form of a diarie and tell something of the Spaniartt's life. He writes of the wrecking of hysse shippe and hysse crude survival on Tearagh't. There is much concerning hysse journie wyth the armada and some word of hysse disposal back to Tearagh't as a prisoner. The diarie gives some detail of hysse lyffe, if you do calle yt that, on that bleak rock. I know not if he surviv'd hysse time on Tearagh't. He deserves to lie in peace, wherever he may be.

Capt. James Morris

These are the translat'd paperes. We found the originales in the driftinge *naomagh*. They were loose tied in a bundle at the stern. I feare they were not in right order. Given some time from mie duties I shall make the translat'd version soe. They are mostlie dat'd. A fewe tell onlie the season, of which yeare I know not for certaine.

Seamanne Shalter

The Spaniartt's paperes

1589 august xxviij

I am broke. It is not the waves, the wreckinge, even mie bones – though some are crush'd. It is mie spirit that lies in ruins. No longer at your side, mie love is all that burns. Mie hand can still write these words. I can listen, in desperate hope, for your voice. I know all is lost. I am soak'd, drench'd as I was on the *San Juan* as we pump'd for our very survival. What was the purpose of so much toyle and sufferinge? What is mie purpose nowe? To die of hunger and cold far from home? Thysse dream I have lived for these four months must end.

Forgive me.

1589 august xix

It rains. Not cold, but endless rain. I see the great island and when the mist clears, the maineland.

Nothing comes. No boats. Only the screechinge of the gulls and the crashing of the waves. Do you remember hearing the waves in sea-shells? The waves here are remorseless, never ending. Through the rain I hear them. I must go mad.

summere

The wind is chill. Soon must be a colder season. Tonight I shall light my fire and cook gull chick.

I am king in a land with no subjects. I eat mussels, chick, boil'd gull eggs. I have no saffron or paprika but I have sac. I shall call a meeting of my council on the next daie. We shall sing and make good cheere.

I lie. I go mad. Alle are dead. Dead. Praie for me.

How can lying here be soe easie. I touch your skinne, you move notte. Our skinne is as one. You raise your head to mie chest. You turn your back and take vino. I watch the curve of your back. You turn again and licke the haires that lie on mie bellye. I am rous'd. I wake. Yt is colde. Mie rock burns wyth cold rayne. Mie face is wet. Teares.

Forgive me thysse sorrow and despair. I shalle die before we can hold each other once more. I know it nowe.

As I write, you sitte still before me. You frowne. There are lines on your brow. You raise a glass. Agua. You are distant – your eyes fix'd on the menne who serve us. You attend to all around you as a cat might. The traders. The youth that attends our table. Anothere frown. Your frowne is your glorie. The meres't concern crosses your face and I am alert to your needs. I love your seriousness. How you eat! Serious again. Anothere frowne as you taste your food. So precise as you take mussels and gambas. You chewe your bread wyth more frownes. A baby cries and you turn wyth concern in your eyes most lovelie. Still you eat.

I love to eat wyth you. To lie wyth you. To eat you as I lie. Rember'st thou that first time? Mie feare was soe great I trembl'd and dranke surfeit terrified that I would not please you. And yet. And yet..... You were kindnesse made manifest. I do believe that I know you lov'd me then. You forc'd me not, mock'd me not (you have since expess'd surprise that I thought you might). After I was spent (so quicke, so soon), I grew again inside you as a young manne might – then I knew our love was fate'd for I was no longere a mere boy fill'd onlie wyth lustful desire. I push'd deep into you, you arch'd your shoulderes as if in pain – nowe I know thysse as your pleasure. I clasp'd you to me and spill'd mie seed again. You saie I groan'd aloud – I remember not though you oft jeste I am most loud in our love-makinge.

You are sometimes quiet. Doth mie noyse silents you? Wolf said that a womanne maketh sound if she breathes through her mouth whils't making love – breathinge wyth her nose alone stifles her pleasure! Your neck seem'd perfect and I lick'd. Your breasts invit'd me and a lick'd more. As I dwelt on your bellye you mov'd your bodie upward and press'd mie head (and tongue) down furthere. Such a taste! Pure but wyth a gentle fragrance – of sexe. Even nowe, surrounded bie thysse endless sea and alone, I grow hard at the memorie.

1588 october xxiij

The tide runs north. Sea crashes against mie rock on all sides. I stare at the course 'tween the great island and myselffe. She rises from the waters as mine own. Green at the topmost, sloping to grey cliffe at the root. There may be caves at the waters' edge – at least there are great black crevasses with that appearance. A strong manne might swim to it if first he survive the fall but the race runs fast and it must be traitorous. Near the island waves crest. But against what? Shallows, rocks, remains of more of our wretch'd and Great Armada? To swim would be to risk being swep't north. Bearable to the flat island but what if I tumbl'd on? There is a headland. Waves send their spray many cubits high gainst the cliffes. The sea would take me, or I would be crush'd in a moment.

A high point rises at the south of the great island. Brown grasses (heather?) traverse these slopes. Nothing moves. Can a land so large have no settlement?

Further south, two more islands. They are as the peaks of our dear picos – but wyth sea drowning half the ascent. Be there ancient trees neath the water – even lost villages? There are certainlie none above sea level. I have never known such bleakness. The islands are as the maineland – cruele, high sided, cliffes topped by naked mountainside. If Adam and Eve were here they need not fear – there is nowhere for a serpent to hide. I am surelie lost. May G-d have mercy.

1588 october xxvij

I look west. How many leagues to the horizon? Perhappes less than one hundred. No land. No sail. On this evening I see storms. Perhappes five at once. The sky is lit orange 'twixt the cloud and water. From the sky fall sheets of rain in great tithes – each fifty leagues or more wide. On mie rock it is dry. I am drinking. For your birthday. By my calculation you are born again thysse very morning. I drink to you, to me, to forget.

Sometimes the waves crest and break in a long line of white – as if pounded upon an unseen shoreline just below the water. But there are no rocks or hidden shores here. Tis a full seven fathoms depth. Then the whole sea to the Easte will be calm – a grey mill-pond. But to the west! The waters never rest. Never even the illusion of stillnesse. Alle is turmoyle.

Great breakers rise from the deep like white leviathans and crash to their waterie graves in an instant. If I am to leave, it can only be east. If I am to die, then I should swim west and be taken to the deep not fifty strokes from land. I think of this and I smile. Forgive me.

1588 nov iij

Mie rock is home to many gull birds, white with black wing-tips. We see not these at home. More majestic are the white, great bill'd birds that do roost in the upper-most crags. By daie they sweep the ocean and glide without ceasing until, like Narcissus, they fall to the waters in a crashing dive. Soundless, deadly. They rise flapping hurriedly, now ungainly wyth their prize – silver, struggling.

Would that I had their wings. I would fly home to you – but first I would take what the sea could give me. I have surviv'd on tiny molluscs in grey – theyr black shells I find below the tide mark. There are mussels also, but too tiny. I tried to eat them with shell intact but retch'd for days, mie guts stabb'd with fire. The gulls' eggs are plentiful. Even the chicks give a little nourishment.

Mie mothere's fathere comes to me. I know not the reason. He was a tarre who claim'd to sail wyth the converso Columbus. Mie grandmothere retained her faith and wyth great pretense sent mie mothere to the church at Lugo. Then scandale. Mie grand-fathere sail'd on a mercantile barque to Venizia. A womanne visit'd mie grandmothere and made claim that he was her husband alsoe. She, an anusim, had a son. Grandmothere wait'd – as you can surelye not wait for thysse poor sowle – but Ben Nahmen dids't not return. She heard rumour that he had anothere familie in the Mediterranie and even anothere in Andalucia. Mothere made jest of thysse for a time sayinge we should visit our cousins in the South. But I thinke she never forgave her fathere hysse waywardnesse. Hysse shame lives wyth me stille.

Despite hysse philanderinge I thought him a good manne. Hysse familie were from Castille and had escap'd the Inquisitores. He was kind and could sing most beautifullye. I think of him as anusim but he may have been meshumadim. Mie mothere once told me that Teresa d'Avilia herselffe was meshumadim so he was in good companie.

I drift in thought. I am close nowe to Teresa's ascetick lyffe. Fewe clothes, what remaynes of mie inke, a knife and a sac of small potatoe (what use shall they be on such a precipice?). I shalle write more the morrow.

1588 july x

We head for Corunna. Somme are lost. Wolf hath heard a fewe lie safe in Vivero. The *Santa Ana* hath disappear'd and the *Santa Maria de la Rosa* hath been de-mast'd. Ruiz Matute commandes the soldieres on the Maria. He is reput'd a cruel manne who lacks patience. He must learn restrainte on thysse journie. Hysse father was a conquistadore. A dog of Cortez who could be command'd to heel or tear the throat of anothere wythout remorse. What must hysse sonne be like? A manne who might kill on command or through lustfull will.

He is a learn'd manne, both in books and the ways of death. Mie mothere tells of menne who are made to feel feare then do the same to otheres. It matters not if those they prey upon are friends – or wyffes. Fear is the lesson they learn and how they must live. There are manie here who commande in thysse ruthless way. Recalde and Sidonia have no such reputation. Bovadillo is one such. A general of great reknowen, he sails wyth de Valdes on the San Cristobal.

Nowe we have surgerie! Wolf is disgust'd, Alonzo outrag'd. "These noblemenne act as though the shippe's provisioninge and custom is onlie for theyr service." One adventuro hath limped since a childe. He ask'd Aramburu for the service of our surgeone and yt hath been agreed. The surgeone shall split the ligatamente – I know not what is intend'd. Wolf wants to be there!

We lie two hundred leagues from Corunna, wyth starvinge and sicke menne around us, scarce agua and rott'd food and mie friends want to attend a surgeone as entertainment. Wolf sayeth the surgeone is paid well – in promises. They are as Felipe's – pledges of gold for a distant daie we shall need G-d's good fortune to see. We go forward to the surgeon's quarters. There are perhappe's fifteen of the hidalgo's menne wyth us. Our noblemanne is utterlie drunke wyth sac, as is the surgeone. Three more hidalgoes are alsoe drunk and I am ask'd to help. Wolf pushes me forward and we grasp our manne's leg.

Now I understand the splittinge of ligamentes. The adventuro was laid to the table and held by a leathere strap. Wolf push'd a leathere bracelet into the manne's mouth but he spat yt out on the instante the surgeone began to slitte hysse skinne. As he rav'd the blade shewed hysse bone and muscle. At thysse hysse brave friends rav'd alsoe, two vomitting and the other running toward the decke. A sinewe was drawne out – the ligamente – and thyss sever'd. Crimson now flow'd freely. As mie mothere might sewe cloth so the surgeone gave thread to needle and drew thysse through the skinne, closinge the manne's knee. All was quiet – if wretching and moaning may be call'd soe.

The surgeone toss'd rank agua o'er the wound and bid me bind yt. He took hysse sac and reel'd to the decke. Wolf look'd on as I finish'd mie task and then smiled, "Perhappes we might try the aire on deck, yt is less rank."

1588 july xx

We are bless'd! Todaie we lay to for an hour at San Anton. All aboard are given a medal. It hath the head of Jesu on one side. Revers'd it shewes the Virgin. T'is inscribed "That I may serve thee". I shall wear it in honour of our love, and Alonzo for the Virgin and infante, Wolf for hysse love of jewelrie.

All have been bless'd at San Anton! The priests have busied themselffes and are exhaust'd. Wolf saies 30,000 menne must be the greatest congregation any church hath seen. I thinke at least half the menne know notte what a church is at all and manie prefere a temple or mosque. They are more impress'd wyth our pay – ten escudos and five taris every month, enough to live like a prince at home.

Wolf asks where we might spend thysse fortune and thinkes menne will gamble it away as they can not send the monnaie home.

1588 nov ix

Mie clothes are now as wretch'd as the poorest urchin's. Jerkin and waist-coat are bleached and torn. Mie shoes? I would tell you I had the presence of mind to don footwear as the *San Juan* sanke. I have none.

My feet are torne by the rocks – scarr'd as if an Inquisitore had visit'd. I no longer notice fresh cuts. I have fallen. Not far. Be not afraid – I can still smile for you and raise my eyebrows as our child would surely like. But there is some mishap to my arm and side. Mie left side is constant cold – even in fayre weather. Mie body is alive with the fire of sun and wind. Mie right side can feel the cold chill at night – it is a sensation mie left knows during the day. Thysse difference between right and left in sensation may kill me yet. To starve, to slake thirst after days of torment, to survive the dreadful fate of mie comrades and yet to die of the cold because I cannot feel it or recognize the need for warmth. Forgive me. Mie pitye goes to you and your family – yt is wasted on thysse poor wretch.

1588, november xij

Nought do change. Yt is as our life at home compress'd to its bar'st details. I thirst – and find water. I hunger – and collect eggs and shells. I am stiff – I stretch. I want what a manne must have and I think onlie of you as I swell and spill precious seed. I need rest – and sleep. I praie. How we complicate these elements in our world.

I am hungrie and must find a serf to cook my food. Certaine things to be eaten only at certaine times. I must wash before and after eating (your father once insist'd I wash during a meal – hath he told you of it?). I must dress – for retiring, for the breakinge of fast, for meeting others. I even wear a hat. Ha! What is the reason for hats when we have hair, though it doe disguise mie yamicka? If I am to have deliverance they will find me without headwear, no shoes and clothes like rags. I shall have gull's egg in my beard. I shalle appear mad.

Time itselffe hath forsak'n me. I know only by the sun that each daie passes. On cloud'd daies morning's moment seems to last until raies of evening moonlight break through. What season is it? The air is no guide. Always cool and wet, the taste of salt everywhere – mie tongue, clothinge. Some cloud cover'd mornings the grey of the sea and sky meet. I see an horizon of a perfectly straight line for hundreds of leagues. Mine eye deceives me notte. The line curveth yet we are taught the sea and earth are flat. Tomorrow I swim west – to be free of this madnesse.

I am cold. Mie left side always so. The hottest sun warms it not. Mie arm screeches to me with the sharpest pains. Tis like being stung many times. But the stinginge continues after the bees have flowen. The palm of mie hand has the constant feel of ice. The right? How can I describe mie right? It is ... just there. Responding to the sun, the sea, all sensation seems as it should be. I feare I have twist'd the nerves and blood vessels of mie left arm and they will never be the same. How can I hold you again? Your faire skynne will be as the roughest parchment to me.

november xiij

I live! I climb'd to the sea and threw myselffe to her mercy. Did I drowne? A memorie came asudden. As the water closed above mie head there was a rushing sound. All should have been at peace but the sea swirl'd around and dragg'd me down in a tumult. Trapp'd air. Foam. A whiteness, more rushing in my ears.

The memorie? I am bathing. You are at toilette and I allow mie head to fall neath the water. When I rise I see you. Smiling. You ask what I am doing and I answer, "Pretending to drowne for Sidonia." You say I am mad.

The tide drew me north some three leagues and the wrecke came beneath me. The *San Juan* shalle save me yet. A mast provid'd purchase and I found – treasures, such treasures! Loose wood everywhere. The waves are making play with our captain's pride. I found rope. I held fast and as I wondered what I must do the tide turn'd. I threw myselffe toward the strand on the great island and swam with all mie heart. It was not to be. I was wash'd to my rock holding tight to the spar and now I must dry the wood for fire. A signal of smoke may save me yet.

1588 november xx

The women! I beg your forgiveness, mie love. I do not mean that in the sense common to our bordellos. Let me tell of the menne in thysse place first. They are strong beyond compare. Most of them look half starv'd. All gristle and muscle. Such sinewes!

Most daies they climb the cliffs for gulls' eggs or carry the weed from the strand to lie on their barren fields. They grow little here. Edible roots thrive in the rocky soyl which must be mercilessly harrow'd and pummell'd to give up its goodnesse. They thatch, carry rock. They row theyr naomoagh into the strait and cross in the rough'st seas, hauling til their backs must break.

They are brown and their skynne weather-burn't as the strongest leathere. They have teeth (some) which they use to bite through their cords and twine. Theyr lips are green from eating grasses.

The sun sears their flesh and seals their wounds. They are as the rock.

The womenne? They are the same. No tender manneres here, mie love. No swirling of pretty lace. The women wear grey or black sackinge. They do all that the menne do and more – for they tend the peate fyres, tidy theyr hearths, cook the meals, wash clothes and look to the children. They haul agua from the well and carry it to theyr houses all daie. Their skin is as brown'd and callous'd as the menne. Quite the youngest of them look soe. I cannot tell those who are still young from those beyond mid life.

The old are bent. Still strong as oxen, still doing the back-breaking chores. But wayward of gait and with more broke or lost teeth. They chewe on food til it is as mush for a baby. They gnaw on bones as would a dog. I admire them beyond anything I have yet seen here.

But I have mov'd on too quicke. I must tell you of my fire. Oh bless'd fire! As I hoped, the wood dried fast in the wind and the rotte had already set in so burning was simple. I sat by it for warmth with no real thought to making a signal. But signal it was! I satte in mie cave falling to sleep when I was stirred. By A VOICE! The voice of a man calling from the crag beneath mie cave. And there he was. Mie rescuer. Hysse vessel – they call them naomagh - was held steadye below by his companions as he scaled the rock to me. I know not his tongue, but I care notte. He beckon'd me follow. Thysse time mie leap was broken by theyr boat. Within an hour I was sitting at a hearth in one of the small dwellinges I had seen from the wreck.

Laughter, some mine, fill'd the hut almost as much as the smoke from theyr fire. There is such joy in being found. I shall live to see our son. I thank G-d in his mercy.

1588 november xxi

Toddaie hath been more restful though thysse is a brutal life. The menne and women toyle from the moment the sun rises. They do not stop. Weariness follows nights of story telling and song and then we all sleep.

In one bed. I am wyth the young boys. Tomas, theyr father, and hysse wyffe wyth the girls. The warmth is fine. The smell is strong but it soothes. There is a constant reek of wood-smoke and peate.

The babes are washed in the sea and they smell of it. Salte is in mie nostrils as I lie.

When it is dark here it is as if someone has put out my eyes. Cloud'd, moonless nights are as pitch. On the rock I dare not move for feare I stumble from my cave to the abysse. Starres are trulye my friend now. On board ship the season'd tarres could tell tales of mighty battles in the sky mark'd by the twinkling lights above. The battles raged for all time they said and only moved a fraction each season – so they could chart theyre course by looking up. To them the night gave hope of safe journey and safe return. On many a night I look'd toward Spain knowing you were there somewhere.

Nowe, I look to the South starre and hope the same. These islanders care little for the starres but they do seem to tell tales of battle – perhaps battles between their g-ds – but I believe they see the battles clearer than I for they call their g-ds by name and wait quietly for an answer. Fynn is one. One of theyr number seems alsoe to be called Fynn. He is taller than the rest – and strong. He smiles often through hysse broken teeth and roars at the tales of Michaele, theyr king.

1588 november xxij

I notice a fewe words of theyr tongue nowe. They point at me and laugh often. They touch mie skinne - rough, but as a new-born's compared to their own.

As the babies fall to sleep in the evening, the menne draw out theyr spirit. They bring yt from the mainlande. It is like aguadiente and it loosens tongues and laughter as quicke as any wine. They make music and song all the while – sometimes a lullabye. At other times the fire is in theyr footsteps and they whirl each other around so that the children scream with laughter and terror. Can thysse life go on? If I drinke more I believe it may last all eternitie.

Thysse world is such a place. Do you remember when we wandered to the hills and looked upon Tui? Such a mighty town could barely be imagined tho you did say you could picture the women washing clothes for their menne-folk – as they do everywhere it seems. But since Tui I have understood that the world is indeed beyond our greatest learning.

Off the coast of Brittannie mie lord Aramburu insist'd we put to anchor and went ashore for cheeses. The people spoke to us in Gael, we understood not but they followed our barter well enough – queso for gunpowder. We tried to tell of Spain – they had heard of it not at all! I do believe they did not even know of their own Rheims, or that they are counted Ffrench. Off Irellanda we followed our lord Admirale to an island they call Inishmore. They knew of us not, had not heard of the Great Armada and knew nothing of Good Queene Bess as the accurs'd English call their monarche.

I discover horizons so long that the earth do curve in appearance, I speak Gael with cheese eaters and now take bread with these rough island-folk. Despite my adventures, thysse world does not even know that Felipe II is on the throne, or where that throne might be – or what possible reason a Spaniard cannot eat pig meat with them, even tho' he be half starv'd.

Even as we lay in in Corunna roads there were menne, if I may call them that, who knew of Felipe, knew a little of the Great Armada (tho not of our cause) but knew nothing of Jewes – other than we are mean spirit'd and worse than heathen Moore. But I could see they had compassion for their kinfolk, could tell the price of rice and might even tell of the guiding star. How can such wisdom go no further than theyr front door?

I rant on the page. But I have been amaz'd at the size and variety of the world and the unknowingness of the people in it. On the bless'd *San Juan* were menne who knew not of the high sierra, could not tell if I were Jewe or Moore (but hated both) and were afear'd for their lives at night because they had shared their bunks at home with cut-throats.

We had one such. Not two days out he fell to fighting on the maine deck with a mid-shipman. The salte mov'd easier than he on the sloping deck but was no match for the man's blade. Afore any could move he had slash'd across the tarre's gut and.....howe he scream'd to see his lyffe flow red from within him. The cut-throat snatch'd – instinctively I think – for the sailor's necklace and silver cross. It was his undoing. He slipped on the spill'd guts of the dying man and was down. Upon him came five or six mid-shipmen and, struggling and kicking for all he was worth, he was thrown o'er the side. He did not swim for long. We saw him sink to his end, blade still held aloft. The mid-shipman was wrapp'd in his bedclothes and throwen to the water with fewe words – but many lice. Neither manne could have tolde why they were at sea, with 500 strangers, on the way to do battle an infinitie of leagues north. Both died ignorant of it alle, their small worlds ended before the wider world could acknowledge them for a moment. Others died of the flux or fever without even gaining deck. For all they knew we were still in port.

I grow morbid. Tis late. The light fails and my new kinsmen are returning. Tonight I shall greet them in their tongue – Dia Gwith. To you I say La Briute and sleep well and safe.

1588 november xxviij

What a day we have had of yt! I went out with the menne in one of theyr naomagh. Trulye these craft can ride the waves. We surg'd (there is no better word) toward the flat island, then swung left direct into the ocean tide. We row'd west some ten leagues til I thought my arms must break and then a calm o'ertook us. We lay for possiblie an hour just drifting as if in a pool. I could see the waves cresting all around, but our course was placid, gentler than a mountain stream. The water was clear and below I could see countless dartinge fish, shole after shole. Eventually, two of the men threw a net o'er the side and we haul'd it aboard, now heaving with silver and grey. One of the menne took the tiller and turn'd us back toward the island. I could see mie rock not five leagues hence. A mighty and stern prison for this poor wretch – now freed.

We row'd again and soon came to the strand. The menne do not use the strand as a harbour. Perhappes there are hidden currents or rocks. Instead they take us alongside some sheer rock-face where they have cut out a slipway, traitorous as ice. What a game it was hauling our catch up the slippe and then across the rocks to theyr houses. The womenne gather'd around and were soon gutting the fysshe. The maineland po-cheen was breached.

We drank. I do believe I sang before I slept. It is now dawn of the following daie. I must rest.

december I 1588

Channukah approaches. It will be the coldest of all my holy daies. The wind here is chill and constante. But when it gusts, my very bones freeze. My left side is still no better. In these winter days the right side joins it in cryinge for mercie from the icy squalls.

I walk'd with one of the children to the cliffe edge thysse morning. We sat looking to the beach they call Coumenole. As we gaz'd the sea grew strong and the breeze quicken'd. Within a few moments the waves crash'd at our perch and all went white. It recalled in an instant the loss of the *Santa Maria de la Rosa* – one moment cresting the waves – the next sunke before our eyes, all drown'd. (Even, I feare, the pilotte's sonne, a ladde barelie fourteen yeares olde.)

Drench'd, I start'd to walk back towards the houses – but could see nothing. We were surround'd bie foame and flying water. We stood still and I offer'd up some prayer. A mitzvah – the air cleared long enough for us to stumble homeward. It should have been easier – all paths lead upwards on this island.

But my senses were swarming and I had concern for the boy. I should not have worried. He grins at me still from hysse place by the fire.

1588 maie I

How mie heart beats. *Santa Ana* has arriv'd. She is huge. More than 1000 tonnes and over 50 guns. Our vice-admirale and true hero of the sea Recalde commandeth. He is basquaise and alreadie a Knight of Santiago. And a relation to the dread Ignatio de Loyola, though I forgive him that. He is an adventuro and a militarie manne turn'd true seamanne. Would he have me for hysse crewe?

The seamenne all wear beards. I would not stand out amongst them though mie skinne is less burn't. The womenne who watch them in the praza dye theyr hair. They are not conversoes. Your fathere suggest'd our son might be a Jesu rather than Jose. It is close enough. I ramble. Yt is the sac. They saie Recalde has never fail'd hysse menne – in the Indies guard or when fighting as Santa Cruz's admirale in the Acores. Hysse commanders and shippes may fail but hysse heart is as a lion's. Old but strong and sure. Lyffe flows through thysse manne. I could follow such.

I must have thee. All seems the same here. But change is upon us. Children play in the praza. Or crie. B'loved Pr de Constitucione. I notice menne as they pass women fayre of countenance. How they do stare, lookinge long and hard. Oft times the women are but children themselffes. Desirous. So wanton. Be they whores? They are womenne surely of faith? Not Jewes. The pleasure carnale is theyre credo. They return the menne's gaze without modestie. Think they of marriage? I feare they do not think at all. They respond as feral cats to the matinge call of the men's gaze. They prowle for mates and mating. Canst they know of love? A love that do surpass the carnale but where the carnale be as natural as drawing breath?

How we made love! You lie. I licke your bodie. I sucke at your neck, your nipples, your bellie with childe. I enter and....what didst thou do? You lay stille. "Shouldst I move?" you asked. "No," I sayeth, "Let me move you." You smile a lyttle as again I enter. You crie out, yet still lay stille. My tongue takes in your taste, from breast to (how you move now!) toes. Your left has more sense than your right. You pull away from my tongue and say it delights too much. I move to your right side, heele, toes. This relaxeth you and you spread your arms. A symbol – no more? – of abandon. Wanton abandon. Your bellie is above me as I licke more. Your breasts do swell, your nipples colour from pale to brown, the roseatte glow grows around each. You arch and presse to my mouth. Your hands do twiste and clenche. You gasp. It disturbs notte mie love. You do not crie out. Not yet. As your abandon growes I know what it is to become one wyth love. My tongue ceaseth notte. You give yourselfe utterlie. And in your abandon you call. Thysse daie you call'd "G-d." G-d is wyth us mie love. He lives through our love and our child.

And after? After is beyond words. You laugh a little. You are calm. You do smile continuous, a smile of rapture. And contente. There hath been no such love as thysse. And I must have thee.

The voices grow around me. One voice calls again and again. They search for men to serve Sidonia. For Felipe I care not. For Sidonia men wouldst die willinglie. I must go. To sea. To fayte? To death?

The manne serving birra moves amongst womenne as a lone wolf. He debuckl'd hysse pantaloons to a dark hair'd wench and call'd her to gaze at hysse manhood! How your fathere would be repuls'd! How our fayth demandeth felicitie. If Sidonia or Recalde shall take me I swear to be faythful though I leave thee. Our love shalle endure til death do part us.

There is a beggare who stands and stares at any

he decides should pay. Yt is a long and hard stare – most discomforting. I doubt he carries a blade but hysse method is to resemble a brigande so that riche menne reach for theyr purse and move on quicke. Hysse skinne is burn'd by sun and winde and he is Gallegan so pure I have heard him speak no othere tongue. Otheres eat vicyualles as he attends. They drink sac and when they can no longer resist they hand himme coin. Has he sail'd wyth Sidonia? Is thysse mie fayte – to beg for the leavings of rich menne in mie own town?

Mie writinge reeks of doom. I have bought a hat! Not a quipa – a real hat. It shall lead newe companions to thinke of me as an adventuro. A manne plays the flute. Thysse can not be develle musique. It lifts the heart and sowle. He has wyth him an angel who collects monnaie from the listeners. She is alsoe in black though her smile is that of a virgin.

I am in mie cups. Yt is dawn. I am decid'd. I shall look on the mercado thysse last time to give me a fond memorie of thysse belov'd place. There is mist as I walk, manie night lights are yet to be dous'd in windows around me. Perhappes menne here have had a last night of love before they saie theyr farewells. The mercado stirs early. Some womenne look at me in surprise as I write. They do not stop as they prepare gamba, pulpo, sardina. They talk to each other as they gut and clean the fysshe. Guts they pull to the side and let fall into buckets. The fysshe are mount'd ready for those who shall buy. An old womanne smiles at me. Busie by habit and happy in nature. She works on nowe cutting the fins and tail from a great silver fysshe. Menne bring in more catch, the fysshe gutt'd in an instante. Pulpo lie wyth legs trailing o'er the tables, theyr black eyes wide and stern. Did they know of theyr fayte as they were haul'd from the sea? Yt is a wonder.

I hear a fysshe wyfe saie that the sierra burns stille. Fires start and beateres come but the sun is cruele and severe thysse summere. No sooner are flames dous'd, more fires appear. How the beateres must run for theyr very lyffes. Yt is time for me to join shippe lest I be tempt'd to forever stay.

Manie are leaving. The lights are gone out and the mist clear'd. The mercado shalle stay, mie poor beggare, the drunkards. They barely know the daie, nor the reason for our sailing. Yt must seem just another war, another desparate adventure to make Spain and Felipe feared throughout the worlde – and rich. Manie here will have sail'd against Drake and Grenville. Do they remember? Dare they think of yt? They will have seen our shippes sunke by cannone, Dutch and Englishe. They deserve rest though theyr dreams shall be full of terror. The gulls call above.

1588 maie iij

I am on board the *San Juan*. There are several of like name. Mie *San Juan* is the *Bautista*. I was taken, wyth gratitude, as a volunteere and have met a fewe more as myselffe. There are at least an hundred tarres and possibly three hundred infantrie, some cavalrie wyth theyr horse and at least twenty adventuroes, mostlie rich menne of leisure I thinke.

These adventuroes. Know'st they love? They strutte as pea fowle. They boast of theyre finery – hose, blaydes, bootes. They (or theyr serfs) carry theyr fine silver and pewter cutlery. The tarres are bare of foot and eat as we do wyth wooden forks and spoons. The hidalgoes talk loud of theyre propertie. A grand house here, a mistresse there, sac that do reste for yeares afore it can be drunke.

They speake not of love, nor the sun and bless'd rayne. Forsooth I believe they thinke that the worlde was for them alone made. To prospere, to robbe, to sow theyre seed so that theyre kin prosper. They shoulds't have a mottoe – I buy, then I die.

Am I cruele? Forgive me. It is hard to watch as they gloate and act as lords – for lords they must be in our dear Spain. They are fayre of countenanace and theyre hands speake notte of toyle. I am no infantrieman butte wythe such men I feel the stronger. I can plant artichoakes and grow from G-d's seed all that he hath given the earth, I can make children and I can love. I do not dare saie I am better than they, yet, is it possible our lives can be as goode in the eyes of G-d? Our deaths will be unremember'd in art and palaces. The love that grows twixt us and in your bellie will certaine live longer.

Felipe sends us to death. Death cannot make me afear'd. These menne live in her shadowe. I understand it notte. Feare is the reason they build theyre palaces knowing the stone will remayne for long after theyre bones are gone. Theyr spirite? Onlie some evil will remayne. The deaths that they do rejoice in. The killings. No love, onlie the darke of theyre soules.

I sytte in conversation with such fellowes and can think only of you and our child. A few talke as if they can controle the weather, the wind, the whims of G-d. Thysse cannot be so. Even I know that beyond les Isles de Cias the oceane changeth on the instante.

Waves rush from calm to mountainouss so quicke our captaines can do little. Yet the administratores talke of plans with the utmost seriousness. The seamenne say little. The soldiers less. There is an administratore here. He holds forth, looks askance and most serious whilst declaiming the need for correct book-keepinge. To not speake drives me to despaire. Butte what can I saie? Mie heart burns with a desire to be wittie at the expense of thysse manne. I know not if he hath faced the sea and her crueltie. To wake with a pale mist onlie to see the shippes disappeare from the horizon in deep'st fog barely a minute later. To watch as soules risk falling from the tops'l or being crush'd by falling timbers. Already have I seen a young hand lose a limb – blood soaked sinewes stretch'd upon the deck. Hysse screaming horrible to hear.

Our administrator can hardlie know of this. He

sits calmly with no awareness that the end of the worlde can come in a moment. Certainlie he talks as if he can bore the wind and waves into submission. He cannot tolerate quiet. No moment of silence can pass – tho it is true the waves drown out most noyse. If we pause for thought he repeats hysse words, encourage'd by some around him. We can be bored by three people at the same time! I find wrath doth rise in me.

To distract me, I rehearse what I might say to the company as I step victorious from my poste, the administratore convert'd by mie wisdom borne of experience. Your father is ever the diplomat that he must sit upon hysse hearte when fac'd with such matters. I begrudge such a skille butte I admire it also. I sitte screaming inside as our administrator asks question after question based on ignorance. Is it possible he knows not the answer to hysse question – 'Why can we not drink sea water at times of drought?' I know of a manne who lived some forty days drinking nought but sea water. The administrator is more simple than that and knows none of these oceane tales. Perhappes we shall test him on brine later.

"We must beware lest we sail to the edge of the worlde," he saies, wyth a most serious expression.

At thysse one tarre can hold hysse peace no longer. “Even Augustine and Aquinas knewe yt is a sphere,” he saies. “And Isidore of Sevilla calculates yt hath a diameter of eighty thousande stadii,” sayeth anothere. “All tread the path of blasphemy,” sayeth the administrator and hysse close companions nod. Soe I find, in less than three minutes, that our administrator is indeed a foole, there are limits to the foolisheness that tarres can tolerate – and I have the same forename as a famous astronomere – though I know notte how far eighty thousande stadii might be. Yt sounds a very long way.

“What of Cosmas Indicopleustus?” saies a seconde administratore, thus far quiet. “Did he not teach that the earth was a great rectangle, bound’d bie mighty walles, the Bless’d livinge above us in a great cavitie beyond the starres.” Thysse frustrates mie seconde tarre again. “We must be careful notte to run into the west wall when we leave Lisboa,” he sayeth, wyth a broad smile. “Dost thou not believe the stories concerninge Presbyter Johannes either?” askes the first administratore wyth a keen look in hysse eye.

“I have seen the lands of whych Johannes speakes,” sayeth anothere tarre. “I have seen the dromedaries, red and white lions, crocodillos and pygmies in the India that he describes. But I have yet to see the centaures, cyclopes and fauns that he claims alsoe live theyr. Nor the phoenix that rises from yts owne ashes. I feare that Johannes tells tall tales – and your Cosmas might do the same."

All is silence. "What say you Isidore?" asks the administratore.

I am sav'd bie a crie from above. We are call'd to decke.

xi maie 1588

A cannone shot! From the *San Martin*. All around trumpets declare that our adventure beginneth. Praie for me. All flie theyr pennantes. Even Drake wouldst flee from such a sight. I can see many galleones. Perhappes fifty. Perhappes twenty urcas and smaller pataches and zabras.

Many shippes are naos, the tarres say they are not true fightinge shippes but merchant vessels from Venizia and Ragusa. They have toweres fore and aft. The tarres say they are too slow and cumbersome for battle. Felipe has commanded theyr presence and saies G-d shall grant us victorie. The stores are astonishing large and various – food for half a yeare. Fifty casks of sardinas and fifty more of tuna! In our hold there are infantrie stores alsoe – shoes, sandales, arquebusses, muskets. We have horse wyth us. Some shippes carry burros to pull the great guns. Nearly 20,000 infantrie are crowd'd neath these decks. It is rumour'd that most have not sail'd before thysse. They praie for calme seas.

All mannere of menne are here, from all the Imperiale lands – even some from Irelannda and some Englishe. Perhappes Arturo Dudley is here. Does't thou remember? He claim'd to be the sonne of the curs'd Englishe queene and begg'd protection from Felipe. I know not if he sails with us to claim hysse rightful crowne.

xij maie

The weathere holds us back. The admirale will not sail in such windes. We lie at anchor at the river mouth with nought to entertain us butte food and wine. Felipe hath provid'd such abundance.

Some menne complain and there is rivalry twixt infantriemen and tarres. The tarres sleep on deck and in the toweres. We sleep below where it is ranke. Adventuros have theyr own quarteres and servants. Servantes to carry the goods administer'd by Cervantes.

Forgive mie jeste. We have onlie humore and wine to keep us calme. We also have almost two hundred friars and priests assort'd. I thinke a rabbi will not be so easy to find.

xiv maie

We rest here stille. We shall not starve. The rationes for a daie are more than many have at home! We are offer'd two loaves. Sundaies and thursdaies there is queso and salt porke (I exchange mie porke for queso and rice). Othere daies we are given sardinas. We have beans and oyle. Agua for cookinge, drinkinge and washinge. Fewe wash. The adventuros onlie I think. They saie the Englishe tarres fare well with theyr rationes – too much birra, salte beefe, fisshe, queso and burro fit for a king. They shall be strong as are theyr shippes.

Each daie hath a watchword. All are taken from Felipe's faith. "Our ladye" is the word for satterdaie. We now have written orders from the Duke. I must keep mie musket clean. Readie to fire. I must not take rationes that are notte mie owne. The ordere ends thus, "No infractione is to be allow'd otherwise offenders will be punish'd at the Duke's discretione"!

xxx maie

The great Armada is join'd. We have set sail! The menne are crowd'd below decks, the tarres above go about theyr work.

june iij

The shippes roll in the constante swell. They sayeth land is seen again. But we are no more than fifty leagues from Lisboa, We should have travell'd beyond Finestra.

We are set for the Islas Berlangas.

june vi

We ride storms to and fro. I feare that we have barely mov'd and make no true progress. The menne are troubl'd. It is darke below decks and some food stinkes most foule. We are told the *Davide Chico* has lost her mast. She heads now for Lisboa. Would that we might join her. I finde myselffe in good companie. Wolfe, a Gironese and hysse young ffriend Alonzo.

Alonzo is of the cavalrie and looks after hysse mare, Laduenda, as a lovere might. He took us to her stall where she looks wyth panic in her great browne eyes until Alonzo approaches and calmes her. Soft words and caresses. A gentle strokinge of her mane. She is most beautiful, a strong horse for carryinge her gallante rider. Alonzo shares hysse food wyth her – tack and grain he offeres in cupp'd hands and she eats most gentlye. Wolfe picks up a leathere sac fill'd wyth agua and holds it for her. Hesitant nowe, she moves her head – first in trust to her master – and now to Wolf. He grins, "I see it is not onlie womenne who I can charm." Not the most modest of menne.

I am unkind. Wolfe is tall, dark and brave. Why should he be modeste unless it be to attempt to disguise a simple truth – that he is indeed most handsome! Wolf has a wyffe and four young children. He declares himselffe the luckiest of menne. He has indeed been bless'd. He hath a fine sense of humore which shall serve us all well on our journie. He knows hysse children to be beautiful – as our child shall be also mie love.

Wolf wears a silver ring. He turns it constantlye, on occasion changing yt to anothere finger or from hand to hand. He is in constant motion. He hath a diet most strange, eating nought but fruit, grain and fyshe. He will not eat meat. On thysse journie hysse diet gives him the advantage o'er manie others as most of the meat is alreadie rott'd. Wolf suffers a little for hysse diet as the fruit is sparse. At least there is an infinitie of fysshe for the taking. He dresses well and boasts of hysse clothes. Hysse tunic cost 100 escudos, hysse boots the same!

He tells me he hath manie fynne boots at home and hysse wyffe chides him that he thinkes he is a womanne at court. He tells how he embark'd on thysse adventure. He heard of Felipe's plans three years hence at the funeral of a young morisco friend. He met two menne who had pledg'd to journie wyth the armada should Felipe's plans be fulfill'd. They had been seduc'd bie the promise of wyffes and propertie in Englande when the curs'd queene is o'erthrowen.

Wolfe hath no limit to what he believes can be gain'd in thysse lyffe and want'd to sail for the pleasure of plunder and journeyinge bie sea. Yet he had n'er sailed before! He saies he swims well but knoweth nothing of shippes. He was sure he would not suffere the sicknesse so common at sea and propos'd the adventure to hysse wyffe. He is perhappes forty though he looks youngere and she was afear'd for him, saieing the armada was a young manne's quest onlie. She listen'd (he saies) wyth great patience until she could stand noe more and said, "You must go!"

Hysse parting from hysse children was sore and yet, and yet.... He sayeth that fewe daies pass'd before his imagination was caught utterlie in the expedition to Lisboa, the beautie of the sierra and new found friends too numerous to name. He makes friends alle the time, where're he may find himselffe. He does so bie attending close to what menne (and womenne) saie. They tell him immediate of theyr dreams and feares. Theyr lives and tragedies are set before him in momentes. He discoveres much so quicke.

He saies to me that he simply finds what we alle know from birth – that menne suffere, we have secret hopes, we feare for our children. We are all the same, whether we are Felipe or the poores't peasant. He offers no counsel, he just attendeth then takes hysse quille and writes what he hath heard. I told him of our unborn child after barelie an hour. He smil'd and declared us bless'd – no chidinge, no suggestion of marriage – onlie a love of lyffe and the gifts that love doth bring.

june x

The winde hath chang'd. We head for Finestra. What madnesse thysse? We have been at sea almost two weeks and had not travell'd north at all. The naos and urcas tack and turn about constantlie. The Armada is slow'd by these falteringe cows of the sea.

A patache goes every two days with letteres to Felipe that tell of our progress. Progress! The food is rott'd and spoil'd. Menne are sicke with it and many choleric. I try to keep mie berth clean but all around menne are disgorginge theyr guts. Chinaroote avails them nought. I cannot walk without feare of treadinge on a comrade or sliding in hysse vomit.

I have met a good manne. Of Felipe's faith. We talk of hysse home and familie. He hath sail'd before and is not ill in the way so many are. He sings to G-d to guide us. A Catalane song that brings a little joy to our foule smelling darknesse. He is nam'd Don Carlos. The same as Felipe's son tho mie Carlos hath none of the deformities of the bodie and witte of the infante. Carlos eats little but talks well and long into the night. We talk as otheres are sicke all around us. The wine de Lamengo is breach'd and we toast our adventure and our loves.

I think our Carlos has many adventures of love. He tells me he has twice been found in the bed of anothere man's wyffe! I ask'd how he defend'd hysse lustful actions to the cuckoldes and he said he had no memorie as he was drunk.

The wyffes seem to have escap'd lightly but what of the menne folk? How might I feel to find you in the arms of anothere? I might watch a little (does thysse seem mad? The shock of mie discovery would remove mie will to move). Then what? Would I crie, "Thou haste cuckold'd me", and draw sabre. Perhappes I would fake a great calme and turn from you both, or rush to your side and beg you to cease? Perhappes I would join you. I occasionallye think of thysse – your lovely body held twixt two menne. But when these dreams come to me, both menne are myselffe! There are no women allow'd on shippe. Othere menne have such dreams. Some grow wild in theyr loss.

Mie memorie returns. A fight. Carlos was unsteady and roll'd into me and my remark (oaf!) anger'd him. He drew blade – where he kep't it I know not – and slash'd across mie forearm. I danc'd back and hit mie head against a beam. In the mist I was taken to a strange place. A wytch and her slaves bath'd and tend'd me and many others too foul of countenance to describe.

I seem'd to drift wyth these creatures for many daies. One was most terribly wound'd and died in great pain, anothere made me laugh and yet anothere just lay quiet. The scene fad'd. For it was all dream and I awoke. In thysse foule smelling hold. Mie fellows around. Mie blood on the boards and Carlos pinn'd by two infantrymenne. He curs'd me, "Jewe dog!" He will be taken to anothere shippe the morrow.

1588 july xxij

Felipe's Felicissima Armada doth appear less fortunate than he might hope. Already menne are drunk and fightinge on the *San Juan*. They say there are near 130 ships. There is enough salt porke to feed our village for eternitie (tho not me!). And the kegs of wine! I miss you alreadie. I praie for us. We have been in harbour a month. Sidonia could wait no longere and now we sail north at last.

I have met a man most remarkable. He keeps neither the Sabbath, nor Shabbus. He dreams of the women he will see as soon as we reach an Englishe port, he fights, swears and every night playes cards til it is too dark to see. Yet he is touch'd wyth beauty. He has such a fair hand. They call him "the poet" – I thinke in mockerie. Yet he does not write poemes. He writes plays – almost all the time that he is not on deck (or dreaming, fighting or gambling).

His playes are fine. He says he has already written a hundred yet he can be no more than thirty years. He writes as if he shall die at any moment and must tell of his heart's desire for every waking second. He sometimes writes a whole scene as we talk and can finish an act within a few hours. He is a Jesuit, born in Madrid and fighting, he says, for G-d, not Felipe. He is called Carpio and allows me to call him Lope. If we call to berth soon, Lope and myselffe must visit the tavernas first to select the best – I jest, I cannot afford the best. He is most bawdy and lewd. He hath great humour and is passionate about hysse work. He does nothinge but write – when he is not drinkinge or sodomizing womenne in porte (so he sayeth).

He tells me that all of G-d's creation is fit subject for verse. A storm brewes – he sketches it in words. The feare in menne's eyes, the turbulent sea, the rolling clouds. All fit. And when we are lash'd bie rain he retreats to some corner and writes on. He knows of thysse fellowe, Cervantes, who has stock'd the Armada. Thysse Cervantes is no Jewe - we have porke enough to stay at sea a yeare. Cervantes writes alsoe – when not in gaol.

He works on a tale of a mad noblemanne – a Don Quixote – who travels wyth a most faythfull servant throughout La Mancha. Thysse work lies dormante and Carpio suggests it maie never appeare to the worlde. I am surprised he doth not finish it himselffe. He sayeth he was noble–born. I jeste notte about hysse writinge. He was writinge plays aged twelve. I was not yet twentye yet Lope could write and aske that hysse work be perform'd in publicke bie noviciandes dress'd as womenne! He calles hysse worke dramatae of the cloake and sworde. There is no lack of such drama here and there shall be more before our journie endes.

I have met alsoe a manne from Cathay. Cathay! Yet he is a gentle manne. He saies he loves hysse wyffe and children and is quiet spoken. Hysse skinne is smooth as a maiden's. If I were drunk I could love him as hysse skinne has the feele of mie love's caress. Perhappes I am drunk. Lope is to blame.

Rua Joachim Yanez. Rememb'rst thou? You laughed, with pleasure so I thought. I wouldst be a writer. "Ah", sayest thou, "a new El Carpio." Now I have the knowinge of him. He whores, he boastes. Sac? Birra? He drinks as a daemen possess'd. I was a daemon. For your love, your fayre sexe. Lugo. Our home. Our daies of love. Haunt'd I lie here. We are but two days travell'd from Corunna. Two days onlie from that safe haven. To be dead wouldst be simpler. "Simple are ye", spake Carpio when he see'st these lines. He thinks me mad.

How I misse our land at Lugo. Your fathere's

olive grove with fennelle, thym and menthe. Artichoakes lay'd in rows in the rocky soylle he hath had work'd by otheres for so long.

Manie here are Gallegan men. Catallanes and Basquaise alsoe. These have theyre cocoaches. It is as woode until agua soak'd. Do these fysshe have human heads as t'is claim'd? If soe, the Basquaise keepe notte the heads. Perhaps they bury them at St Jean. They presse it wythe garlicke and oyle to make baccauloe. Cook'd and stirr'd to a soupe it is a princelye repas to mayke the bread edible and the heart singe. There are some jewes mongst the Catallanes. Anusim from Girona. They live wyth Christianes, Moors and Morisco in great tolerance! The Basquaise know alsoe manie conversoes. They call them chocolate makeres.

We eat the bacaulloe afore milke be added. The tarres have named us bacaloose which they thinke most wittie. They gorge on porke. The slaves share our repas in silence and fynde it pleasinge enough. We have mielle. Howe it sweetens the evenings.

There are manie slaves. Moste have sail'd butte once onlie – brought across the great oceane to be herd'd as cattel. We smelle theyre feare. The soldieres make playe with them and caste some poore devilles to the waves for sporte.

Can'st thou bear mie ramblings. I thinke of you and our unborne sonne as a treasure to be earn'd. Shalle we name himme Jose? Not Jakob as mie fathere do desire. It would not please our lord at Lugo. Mie newe friends jeste our childe should be named Israel. They know notte our Lugoanne princelinge and hysse hatred of converso and jewe alike.

There is much talke of Frobisher. A greate admirale. He will have seene not a fleete such is thysse. We approach la Rochele, a fynne porte. Many shyppes lie there. Some galleones and manie cogs and barques. The captaine hath spake wythe a French officer who might change sac and bread for muskets and shotte. Now we shall have chamois on boarde. They are as afear'd as the slaves and do shitte alle the tyme.

I have seen the moste beauteous mappe. Mayde for Felipe himselffe by Agnese. It showeth greate fysshe off the coaste of Englande and some mightie galleones. I know notte if the galleons shalle be there and have not yet seen fyshe close by, greate or small.

july xxiij

There is a manne here who dies with the cancre. He hath been sudden tooke. On our first daie he laugh'd with the tarres and adventuroes, delighting in the rush of winde on his face. Now hysse skin is cold to the touch and he speakes little. He asks onlie for agua and calles out in pain occasionallye. What can such death teach? That all lyffe is precious and temporarie. That death comes when she chooses and spares notte old or younge, rich and poor.

Thysse man is rich. He has seen o'er all our belov'd Spain and did serve at court. He has known manie women and had a wyffe and growne children. He sail'd wyth Sidonia to the Acores and surviv'd perilous winde and mighty oceane waves. Does he think of thysse as he dies? He calls onlie for agua. I think he feeles onlie the growing cancre and wishes an end to his pain. End it shalle. Then he will be caste to the sea wyth otheres that have died – some starv'd and more from disease or accident no fault of theyr owne. All will feed the fysshe to be reborne. Perhappes he will come again to Spain as baccallou.

Forgive mie morbid thoughts. There is solace in

knowing that we can never die absolute. They say a dybbuk may come at the pointe of death so that we may continue and finish the unfinish'd work of a wandering soule. Perhappes in torment, perhappes joy. You have work unfinish'd – the protection of our son. Mie work may be done – I know notte.

These menne! Alonzo burs't in to our quarteres wyth great smiles and acclaim sayinge one of the Portugaise hath nett'd a shole of squid. Wolfe and I have been on decke and the creatures are as octopus but more varie'd. There are two the size of young children – white, purple and glisteninge. Theyr eyes are enormous and black as coals. The legs – Alonzo calles them tentacles – are two paces long and cover'd in suckers – pink and round as a babie's mouth. All can be eaten. Those that eat notte thysse food of the sea will miss a fynne feast (sayeth Alonzo – I am not so sure).

There are several smaller squid that our Portugaise friend alreadie prepares. First he holds one just behind the eyes and twists. He draws the head slowlie and alle the insides follow in a white masse. He saies it is possible to eat these guts alsoe but he doth not recommend it as the body is so plentiful. Wolfe steps forward. Is there no end to thysse man's talents! He grasps something under the neck and draws out – a quille! "Nowe we needs't not go short of quilles and inke," he saies. You shalle not believe thysse next. Dragg'd wyth the guts is a small sac – of inke! Wolf dips hysse new-found quille into the inke-sac and writes, "Not bad for a landsmanne." Nowe Alonzo eats the tentacles wythout cookinge! He offeres me a small tapas.

I feele a true tarre. I write thysse wyth squid quille and inke and have eaten the raw flesh. It tastes and smells of little – perhappes salt water onlie. It could keep a man alive. "It goes well wyth wine," sayeth a nowe drunken Wolfe. I believe he would eat a dog wyth enough wine. The menne watching have not eas'd theyr nausea much. The watching makes it worse.

Thysse adventure shalle change us alle. I have alreadie seen more death than at home. But it is the lyffe that we behold every daie that inspires. The Portugaise, the Basquaise, more dark skinn'd fellowes than in all of Galicia. I have eaten squid uncook'd. I have seen such mightie waves and menne clamberinge the masts as children might swarm through the branches of trees. The sunsets! The sicknesse. The terror. The disgraceful deportement of the princes. And theyr conduct is fill'd wyth disgrace. Some have twentye or more serfes. They weare theyr jewel studd'd jerkins as at court. Theyr menne weare onlie rope sandales and live in feare lest they should displease theyr masters. The serfs have more tales to tell than theyr princes. Of love (I love you), ffreindshippe, lyffe below decks, the sierra at night. Yet they may not speake to theyr masters untille theyr masters first saie a word - "Get me thysse. Take off mie boots. Prepare mie bed." It disgusts me.

Doth Felipe himselffe trulye understand anything of hysse worlde? Or does he onlie echo the words of Columbus – "trulye for gold a manne can take hysse sowle to paradise." Shall Felipe enter paradise though onlie hysse golde? Does kindnesse count for nought. Wisdom? Generosity of spirite? Felipe visits wheresoever he pleases but who does he meet? Princes? Menne of business? Papal envoys jewel-encrust'd as at hysse court (though he himselffe is reknowen'd for more simple dress). Underlinges that dare not speake? Do palaces bring paradise or pain? I need noe palace. Onlie your hand, your bellie, our sonne and the joy of listening to the tales of ordinarie menne. These tales bring companionshippe that shalle last.

Thysse adventure shalle change us alle. I shall love you always though I know not who I shall have become bie my returne – if G-d grants me safe passage. Mie fathere talks little of hysse wars and the deaths he witness'd. I should have listen'd closer as he mumbled about ffriends that died and the companionshippe to be found in service to the king. I know nowe a little of what such companionshippe can mean. I would, I think, die for Wolf – and perhappes him for me – yet we have knowen each other but a fewe weeks. He has opened hysse sowle to me wyth no shame, nor hesitancy. In thysse frankness is to be found the heart of frienshippe and love.

I imagine it would be possible to find such in anyone if you have patience. Imagine taking a wyffe from Cathay or the land of Cortez. Such a wyffe (or husband) would bring all the local customes, her familie, a new language, a new understanding of food and habits of eatinge. A new way of making love! Such a stranger could entertain a spouse for a lyffetime – if that spouse was open to learning. Even understanding another's speech could bring interest and passion to such a marriage – Wolf saies that the tongue of our enemie is barely possible. "Gracias" becomes "Thank you" but not one of us can say ought but "Sank you". Thysse has a quite different meaning to the Englishe, a meaning more in keeping wyth theyr attempt to destroy the invincible armada!

July xxiv

The cancre has finish'd yts work. Menne gather to say prayers and mourne our companion. Such countenances. Sorroweful yet burn'd with the sun and to a degee full of the lyffe that the sea brings – the joy of the waves and the might of the winde.

These menne grieve yet through theyr grief they shewe little but lyfe. They are all adventuroes – not as lords, but adventuroes of the land, the sea, theyr caserios in Spain, the lyffe to be found in the sierra and the soyle. And in theyr loves. I praie thysse adventure is brieffe. How can menne of the soyle survive yt? Theyr work is in theyr fingeres, hands and the back-breakinge task of turning the earth for crops. I doubt they thinke of yt as work. Yt is just the way they live. But nowe they must rest, await a lessening of the seas simplye to see the sun that they know as that whych gives lyfe to theyr planting. To be away from such toyle for a fewe daies confuses and disconcertes them so. If we are away for manie weeks as hath been suggest'd they shall go mad wyth apathie and the lack of satisfyinge work. To work for them is to exist. Wythout such labour they have noe joy. I feare that those that finde theyr worth onlie in toyle on the land, the love of theyr families, even musicke shalle soon despair of thysse great adventure.

satterdaie

Wolf sayeth I shall never write as doth Carpio or himselffe. I should write from mie heart (a difficult task when it lies in Lugo). Does your lord still pursue you?

I think of thee tho I am distract'd. By the stinke, the lonelie miserie of the menne as they crie out for agua, for home and theyr lov'd ones. The cries are not always aloud. I see agonie and despair in theyr eyes. If thoughts of death were not a sinne for them I know they wouldst seek it rathere than face more of thysse great adventure. I miss your skinne. They must miss so much more – agua that is fresh, the winde in the sierra, the precious rain. I know I shall feele these again. I praie I shalle soon feele your skinne close to mie owne once more. If you find anothere I shalle understand. I shalle lie with the knowledge that you are caress'd and have happiness. I forgive any manne who brings you such, tho I be torne by jealousie.

I thinke of you wyth your lord and mie gorge rises. He loves thee not though he covets you – as a prize. He collects too much – serfs, lande, menne in bondage, silver and gold. He hath more titles than all but Felipe and a fewe grand courtiers. Nowe he wants to add your name and body to hysse collectinge. Even as I write I know I shalle not ask you to resist him. If he offeres our son a good name you must take it. There is no shame in sacrifice for our children.

I write and mie heart breaks. I shall be more careful wyth Wolf's easily proffer'd recommendations. He saies I report too much – the simple food of the Basquaise, the terror of the sea for so manie that have not seen such waves and tides. I can even tell of the exacte passage of our journey in some detail as Wolf hath "borrow'd" the shippe's log – no doubt from the same place he stole Agnese's beauteous mappe.

From our captaine's log

Satterdaye The xxvth daie, At Middaie we wente till xij the next daie Ne & b[y] e. 31 L.

Sonndaye. The xxvjth daie. At Middaie we wente till xij the next daie ENe. 36 L.

Monndaye The xxvijth daie, At Middaie we wente till xij the next daie eNe, 32 L.

Tewesdaye The xxviijth daie. At middaie we wente till iiij of the clock in the morninge eNe, 20 L. at what time we espied a saile going to the westwards and so tacked with her & havinge but litle winde till Middaye NW & b N. 3 L. & could not speak with her.

Wedensdaye The xxixth daie. At Middaye we wente till xij the next daie N. 19 L.

Thursday The xxxth daie. At Middaie we had foggie weather wente till xij the next daie N. 4 L. & N & b W. 4 L. & e & b S, 5 L. & eNe 5 L.

FFRYDAIE The xxxjth daie, At Middaie we wente

till xij the nexte daie Ne & b e. 14 L. & eNe. 20 L.

(*July 1588*)

Satterdaie. At Middaye we wente till xij the next daie 36 L. eNe. Vicyualls Remaining are followeth, viz Meale. Barrells 39. Stockfishe 2081 coples. honie 4 firkins & 5 Barrells. Sweete oyle 3 Barrells, Oatmeale 20 Barrells. Peas 20 hoggsheads. Rize vinegra 1 hoggshead.

I trust that maketh our journie cleare to thee! It lies easier wyth me to tell of such things for in mie heart I am mortale afear'd. Thysse journie is an Inquisitore of the sowle wyth no need of help from the menne of Loyola. I feare I shall not return. That Wolf shalle be kill'd as manie adventuroes before him – far from theyr lands and theyr loves but giving theyr lives for a greater cause – that of pure spirite. A love of lyffe so great that they offer yt in sacrifice every daie.

I am surround'd bie menne who die of fever, who groan and spewe vomit even as they drink agua. They are the ordinarie seamenne who have no choice in theyr travails. Anothere died thysse daie, mewling in pain as would a new-born kitten.

There was little ceremonie. Wrapp'd in hysse spew-cover'd cloak he was taken to the decke and caste quick to the sea. No prayer, a fewe words, then on wyth our great quest. Hysse sowle flies to Spain wyth the gulls that flie o'erhead.

July xxvij

Mie morganne davidde is lost! I know notte which is worse – the loss or the nature of it. One of the tarres did wager the next land we couldst see would bee to porte. I sayeth starboarde. Certain it seem'd. We are headinge north and theyre can be no land to porte unless it be America. Butte land there is. Call'd Isla de Re, no more than five leagues from La Rochelle. It is cover'd in olive groves, the trees leaning to the grounde, blowen by oceane wind. It hath notte the mountains of Illas de Cias so I coulds't see it notte. May mie star of Davidde bring my victor good fortune.

August ij

Thysse is quite remarkable. Volunteeres were

requested last night to manne a patache to take a womanne from the *San Salvadore*. A womanne! Yet alle knowest there are no womenne permitt'd on thysse journie.

Of course Wolfe was first to volunteere. For curiositie onlie he saies though Alonzo and myselffe suspect'd othere more base motives. We took the patache quicke to *San Salvadore* to hear a most curious tale. Perhappes Wolfe will be sated in thysse knowledge. A gunner's wyffe hath been secreted on board as the captain's mistress and she was wyth childe. I know not whether she be cuckoldinge her husband (a brutish Dutchmanne) but she was most certainlie pregnant!

Alonzo and myselffe helped her to our small boat while Wolf looked on in a sulk. Even he shalle not be imagining making love tonight for our good ladye was alreadie in the first pains of birth.

"What nowe?" ask'd Alonzo. Wolf thought we must either take her back to the *San Juan,* take her to land or throwe her o'erboard! I hope he was jesting about the last. We are now familiar wyth the Englishe coast and the decision was made to attempt land. I know not what might have happen'd had we been tempt'd to return to the *San Juan*.

We found ourselffes heading north for the lights on the Englishe coast notte thirty cables distant. We were not accost'd and beach'd our poor craft close to the river-mouth. Alonzo said thysse was Dartmouth. No more could be discuss'd as the womanne's pains were now quicke and severe. She cried out as we carried her to the shingle and then sat down to await her fayte.

"It falls upon us," sayeth Wolf. Alonzo look'd aghast. I guess'd not what was intend'd. "Have you done thysse before?"

"No, butte canst a thinge that womenne have perform'd for soe long be so difficult?"

I understood. Thysse manne of manie talents now was to become a midwyffe. The womanne took pause in her cries and sayeth to Wolf, "It shall soon come. You need onlie attend at the last and turn the baby as he comes forth."

The blood! Her grevious cries! And most wond'rous to see – her sleep twixt the most ferocious of her pains. For a full five minutes she would heave and turn, twisting her legs and opening them a fraction, then far wider. Then quiet would overcome her and she would sleep. Sound and deep t'would seem. All thysse on the hard shingle wyth onlie Wolf's cloake for comfort and nought for modestie. Alonzo was transfix'd. He would stare at the womanne's eyes, twist wyth her in her labours and urge her to press harder for the baby's sake. A deep crimson cover'd her thighs and then....then. Such a show of blood and urgency as she cried out and seemed to force the child from her. Wolf twist'd the baby as she had ask'd and there he was! A perfect boy (whether the son of a gunner or captain I know not).

"Give me your blade," sayeth Wolf to Alonzo, then deftly cuts where child and mothere are join'd. The child cries, Wolf grins, Alonzo is overcome wyth weeping. I am amaz'd at G-d's grace.

"Gracias," saies our new mother whose name we do not yet know. And 'tis done. We are merely three members of an invadinge army, nowe ten leagues from our shippe, wyth a new-borne child and a womanne exhausted bie her night's work and no thought but for her safety.

"Time for a birra," grins Wolf and walks toward the lights.

T'is quiet. A taverna (forgive me). Yt requires little to make true friends in thysse lyffe. Attention to the sadnesse in the eyes of strangers or the joy as they walk tells all you need to know. To listen for but a brieffe time, carefull and respectful, will offer even more. Sitting at cardes I fynde Alonzo loves fruit and longs for Englishe mulberries. At hysse hearth, a newe friend Padraig syttes, as I sat for mie grand-mothere, turning yarn for hysse womanne while she knittes a jerkin. Wolf, who plays cardes like a daemon, told me yesterdaie he offers prayers to trees! "All G-d's creatures," he saies.

A womanne sittes near who cries quietly. I know not what afflicts her soe. Her tale will not be newe – a lost love, a friend's death, a tarre lost at sea. As I write Wolf approaches her and offers solace (Padraig glances at hysse cards). I fear a rebuff. There is none. Her face fills wyth lyffe as Wolf talks. He returns (glancing at hysse ruffl'd cards). "What ailes her?"

"I hope hysse answer will not be too disruptive to our game," whispers Padraig, "Hysse hand is shitte, mine is better."

"She tripp'd as she came in and has a sore toe," sayeth Wolf.

"A sore toe?"

"I have offer'd to bathe it later," he smiles. "I thinke we should call for more ale. The cards are not soe kinde thysse night."

Therre are fewe tarres. I drinke crush'd navarres! And a birra call'st Devonne Summer. Cutlasses are kep't tied to the walls. Thysse is a warreing place. I am not asked mie name or shippe. None suspect I am a midwyffe. The tarres awaite theyre admirale. T'is Drake himselffe. What kind of foolhardinesse is thysse enterprise?

A fewe from *San Salvadore* lay wyth locale women thysse last night whils't others drank wyth Drake's men. Soon shall we try to kill each other at our captaine's command. I have seen the Englishe quarrel with each other allowing our men to go freelye amongst them. Yet tomorrow or the following daie we shall be at each others' throates as dogs turned against deere. I have seen quarrels in the streete 'twixt Englishe menne too far in theyr cups to stand. One was kill'd as he lay hurt. Noe Spanniartes are soe fayted thysse daie. The Englishe lose menne to theyr owne, to sac, to birra and the blade. We Spanniartes cheer notte. Our time is at hand – if there are Englishe who doth remayne living to sail and fight.

We are join'd bye our newe friend, an Irellandamanne. From An Dingaen - Padraig de Barra. He is tall, like Wolfe though wyth more weather'd countenance. He seems drunk but is happy enough to meet wyth us and share our repas. He offeres us tobaccoe from a pipe that he draws on constant. Hysse arm is cover'd in tattoes. Some seem to lie in the skinne itselffe. Wolf whispers that he was probable born wyth them. "Do you like tatooes?" sayeth Padraig in the Englishe way but wyth a trace of difference. 'Like' comes out as 'loike'.

"I do", saies Wolf and soon they are deep in conversation. I see Padraig glancinge constantlie around. He is suspicious of somethinge. Capture? Betrayal? I know notte. Padraig leans forward – a reek of tobaccoe and spirit comes from him. And alsoe a fyner smell. The smell of honest toyle, the earth. He must be a farmer. He turns from Wolf. "Will ye take me wyth you?" he saies.

Alonzo is startl'd. "Why?" "Because the she tyrante shalle not have me fight against the true fayth. I would rather die alongside Spanniarts." Alonzo is much taken wyth thysse. I say, "Thysse great adventure is no more than Felipe's pride and folly. If he were a jewe G-d would have alreadie cast him aside for hysse pridefullnesse!"

Alonzo glances at me and continues, "It is but seven yeare since Felipe seiz'd the throne and lands of Potugale yet even hysse mottoe for our venture reeks of hubris – Exurge Domine et Vindica Causam Tuam – indeed. Why should the Lord arise to vindicate a Spanish king's cause?"

Alonzo is most agitated now and Padraig looks alarm'd.

"We have the greater tradition – of conquest, of navigation, even of holie warre in G-d's name. Were Da Gama and Columbus not Portugaise? We set sail from Lisboa - a Portugaise harbour."

Wolf grins, "Perhappes we should speake a little loudere, there may be one or two here who do not yet know that we sail for Felipe. How can we smuggle Padraig to our shippe?"

"I shalle not make the Invincible Armada vincible," Padraig saies quietlie wyth a smile. "I feare it is alreadie soe."

Carpio said the invincible Armada is akin to jousting with windmills. Our tercios would be caught up and throwen to the winds. Padraig hath more trust in our menne though he trusts not the Englishe at all. He was at Smerwycke when we were trick'd to surrendere, then slaughter'd by the Englishe. Manie were trapp'd in the fort and parley'd for safe passge onlie to be kill'd to the last manne.

Thysse tobaccoe is strange indeed. I am not oft

bored – so much work, so much writinge. But if boredom comes I shalle light a pipe and thoughts do fill mie head.

I am compell'd again to write as I feele – mie losse for you, mie longinge to see our sonne. I see clear the lyfe all around – trees, floweres, the smiles of womenne, the rough talke of tarres. I see G-d in thysse lyfe and praie yt shalle continue. Wych yt must. When we are but rott'd corpses, the birds shalle sing stille and clouds shalle roll with the winde.

Padraig asks what I write. He reads notte. I tell him these last words. "You are a morbid Jewe, I see all that you see but dare not think of death. You think onlie of death. You have surviv'd whilst others fell. Do you not carrye theyr cries and blood with you now?"

He smiles a little. "Why not carry a tankard to the landlord? He shalle help us both forget."

I take the tankards and returne to find Padraig deep in conversation with anothere. I sytte and feel I shoulds't write. A manne wyth verilye the longest hair I have yet seen offeres me a quille. And inke! In a mere taverna – perhappes the influence of Carpio is spreadinge even here. It makes him no less clumsye as he spilles mie drinke before returning to pour more. In mie lonelie madnesse I watch the door for you. A manne enters wyth hair dyed as a woman might – ochre wyth shades of red. Anothere is here. A woman thysse time. More ochre. Do they wish to appear as sand upon the shore? A group nowe. Three menne, one most sombre in black. One most animated. Talking wyth hysse companion. A womanne (not you mie love, you are far from here though in mie heart). She is dress'd in black (most rare) and hath lit some tobaccoe. She reads as she walks.

Wolf points to her and smiles. Thysse man hath no shame (he is, after all, not a converso) – he rises and goes to her. They are quicke talking. Of the weather – as in the Englishe custom? I think notte. What fowle tricke of the light is thysse? A manne opens the door who I know. Dress'd most strange. He struts as a proud Englishmanne yet I am sure it is Faji – head-dress, striped gown, long beard, great grins from hysse brown face. A veritable Diaz de Vivar. I shalle go to him if he sees me notte.

Wolf returns fluster'd and before I can signal that Faji is here he asks if he may read mie scrawl. He casts hysse eye o'er mie shouldere but saies little. I said, "I shall consider it." To which Wolf repiles, "Then I consider it done" and, "Let me contribute to your poor diarie" He writes thus: Mie greetings to you and your soon to be born child. I try to distract Isidore from hysse thoughts of you wyth as much wanton carousinge as is possible. I feare that he is too smitten – not a manne possess'd but certainelie one whose heart cries out for its sowle's mate.

I watch him now as his eyes scan the room, not for inspiration but for yet more distraction from hysse sorrow. I shalle not crticize him as I know too well thysse loving mourninge where all reminds him of hysse love – the sun becomes the Spanishe sun, a taverna a place of memories – people look familiar though it cannot be so. I doubt if these women remind him of you. They are a rough sort and good in theyr way. He returns, I must bid "adieu."

I touched my Moor's coat and found it was not Faji. Perhappes mie eyes see what they want to see. I cast them o'er Wolf's scribblings. What shall I call thysse? An interlude? A distraction? An impertinence – he writes of mie grieffe. And yet I dids't invent Faji as he sugests grieffe shall. Hysse words are both kind and cold. He looks deep into mie soule and reports that which he finds as a manne might comment on a corpse. I am more alive than Wolf's words convey. Am I harsh? I read again and detect a sympathie. I shalle permit him to buy more birra so we may drown our sorrowes in harmonie.

As he returns to the bar I notice a slipp of parchment on the table. It holds the first fewe lines of a poem, badly writ though wyth some promise. It is in Wolf's hand –

Those lines that lines that I before have writ
do lie,
Even those that said I coulds't not love
thee dearere,
Yet then mie judgment knew noe reason why
Mie most full flame should afterward
burn clearer.

He returns and sees the scrap. He crushes it wyth an insousciant look and casts it to the floor wyth noe further ado. "Let's drink."

"But what of your verse?"

"Twas a brieffe passion. These things deserve noe recording in verse. In any case yt was copie'd from that fellowe." Wolf indicates an Englishemanne much in hysse cups.

"Kyd's labour," saies Wolf, "A sadnesse it is not mie own," and turns back to hysse drinke.

Some of the Englishmenne in our taverna are the fattest menne I have ever seen. Thysse claim would include the friar who bless'd our journie and could not climb from the *San Juan* because of hysse surfeit of.... what? Wine? Food? Had he fallen to the sea we could have tied him to a rock as a warning to alle shippes.

These Englishe sitte wyth thought onlie for food. How they yaw and roll when they walk – like a womanne wyth child, or a barrique. One such has a great tattooe on hysse forearm. A dragon wyth knight. Santa Georgio himselffe perhappes. He rolls into Wolf as he walks. "Now there'll be trouble," sayeth Padraig. Indeed I see Wolf rise, anger'd and closing hysse fistes.

"I call'st thou fat," I hear him say to thysse manne two times the size of the taverna door. Our own drunken Englishemanne glances up, hysse eyes full of alarm. He is bewigg'd though not the powder'd wigge of the gentlemanne. Hysse wigge is cut short and dyed to appear hysse owne hair. It is a type of modestie. Though not the modestie of our brethren who covere theyr head before G-d at

Shabbus. Indeed I thinke thysse kind of wigge is in some part immodest. It is made to make the manne look youngere by hiding hysse baldnesse. Wyth that he hopes to attract womenne. He seems attractive enough to mie eyes. Hysse conceit shall lead to the tarres making play wyth him. Thysse may be the reason for hysse quiet.

Oh! Wolf has push'd hysse giant against mie bewigg'd creature and both sprawl on the sawdust. I can see mie manne's legs jutting out from under the tattoe'd manne's body. He moves hysse feet and I see a hand weakly rais'd above the fat one's shoulder. Two menne heave the oaf from the floor and there doth lie mie little bewigg'd gentlemanne. 'Cept hysse wigge is no more. There are some wisps of hair on hysse otherwise bald head and the wigge lies on the floor where yt fell. A shout is made. And anothere. Some menne point at mie poore fellowe and I feele mieselffe mov'd in pitye. I go to him, help him to hysse feet. I knowe notte how injur'd he is. He groans a lyttle when standing.

"Thank you," he saies, simple and sad.

"You have left your work," glancing at mie writing. Mie work! I am nowe recognized as a writer! How easily we move twixt roles in thysse life – infantriemanne, friend, fathere, lover, enemie and nowe a scribe.

"Can I help," saies mie man. "Mie name is Kyd. I write a little myselffe." Kyd pulls from hysse jerkin what resembles a play. I tell him yt is most beautiful writ, the strokes curving across the page. "Tis childe's work when compar'd to mie friend, Marlowe. He hath creat'd a daemon of the stage – Faustus – yt shalle be play'd long after we are dust."

I ask if Gato or deBaena are knowen. Kyd shakes hysse head. "Hey Alonzo. Come and look here, we have a writer wyth us."

Alonzo walks over and settles wyth Kyd to talk. They laugh a little before Kyd takes hysse leave wyth two womenne also much the worse for drinke. These poets and play-writers seem to have no thought of vice othere than as inspiration or adventure to be record'd. Kyd should take care. Not all such menne find appreciation for theyr art.

More from the fleet are arriv'd. In a patacha? They walk to the bar as menne might who live locallye and I see others close bie move away, some glancing at the dress of theyr visitors wyth curios expression. Thyss may not end well.

Wolf is in deep conversation nowe wyth Padraig

and seems impress'd - I doubt yt is wyth our new friend's learning. I see him take a quill and begin to write. "Thysse Padraig is a manne of the soyle. It is something I admire greatly though the art hath escap'd me."

Wolf places hysse writinge before me on the table. It is in latin and he quietly translates: "I wouldst rathere be on the soyle, a serf to anothere. To a manne wythout lot whose means of lyffe are not great. Than rule o'er all the dead that have perish'd."

"You?" saie I.

"Plato" he whispers wyth a kindly but still mocking grin. Padraig might be surpris'd to ffynde himselffe such an inspiration.

Eveninge

Our newest arrivals are taken to Dart castle. Soldiers enter'd, fast surround'd them and march'd them out. No struggle was made. No great noyse. And all quicke return'd to taverna lyffe – drinkinge and conversation. Barelie a glance to the door they had been led through – a back door that seem'd onlie to go into the alleye. One fellowe remark'd they were to go to the castle and a few exchang'd looks that gave away nought. I know notte if they be kill'd or are nowe safelie hous'd.

Three castles guard the sea – Dart, Totnesse and Berrie Pomeroi. Dart is built by Hawley, a merchantman long dead. It towers above the cove at the entry to the porte. Festoon'd wyth cannon and wyth a chain for trappinge any shippe that ventures toward the porte. Felipe is wise not to plan landfall in these parts. I hope the menne are safe. Thysse wouldst be a lonelie place for a Gallegan jewe and a fewe comrades.

Wednesdaie

The menne are return'd. They have been royallie entertain'd by theyre newe friends, the Englishe tarres. These suffere the memorie of the Scots queene kill'd at Fotheringaye, since but a little o'er a yeare. They sayeth the axeman held high her head and hairwigge part'd soe the people couldst see the shayme of age and baldnesse. No beautie remain'd. Her sowle had flowne, as her dancinge feete didst flie when younger.

The menne have been told of anothere Castillo

on the North coast some leagues from here. It is call'd Tintagella, the home of Arturo. He was a greate magickan with a mightie blade and beauteous wyffe – alsoe kill'd. For love.

Thysse place is cold. Yet manie sytte drinking outside the taverna in the winde. I know not how they suffere it. I sitte not far from some fine gentlemenne and womenne and can hear theyr speech. Theyr manneres are most curious. Menne swear and curse in theyr cupse. They paw at younger womenne that serve at table and will occasionallye follow a wench to the alleye where her cries (of rapture or pain – I know notte) are soon heard. Yet wyth theyr wyffes they seem most considerate. They pull back chairs as theyr womenne sitte. They cossette them wyth fine speech – "Mie ladye thysse and that." They are most carefull wyth theyr rapieres and almost dance to theyr laydies' biddinge.

Thysse same evening they will change theyr clothinge and enter the taverna seeking anothere kind of dance. I can hear alle that they say as they sitte in the sun and breeze. The womenne use the same figures of speech as the rich menne – a polite "such a shame" or describing all and sundrie as "lovelie". I suspect that if these same ladies hear of theyr menne's night-time excursions they will say onlie, "Good lord, what a shame," and will turn the conversation again to, what? Politickes? The weather ("T'is hot for the time of daie. Not as hot as thysse time last year"). The fayte of theyr virgin queene? More likelie other locale gossip.

I thinke local tales say more about the fayte and customs of menne than the grand histories that shall be writ about these times. I have already o'erheard tales of an older womanne that marrie'd a younger (Harrowe) manne. I know not what is meant by Harrowe. I hear he hath "good manneres" and is "no foole."

I hear of anothere who wanders forlorne wyth no wyffe. He was adopt'd by newe parents and taken in to a rich family but hysse new mother and father were too aged to understand him at alle. He is "lovelie". I hear of a womanne who mourns a husbande long since dead but she canst find none to match him. Thysse gossip seems to be the stuff of lyffe. Little may be learn't from grande declarations.

What shalle be told of our armada – 30,000 menne, 200 shippes, manie weeks at sea? Compare such wyth the tales of ordinarie menne and womenne who love and lose, watch as theyr children play, walk six leagues merely to buy bread.

The tarres here are barefoot – a fewe in sandales of straw. None weare hose. A woman hath with her a child of no more than two yeares. She doth talke to her all the time. The childe talks alsoe. Perfectlie. The menne talk of a game. Call'd boules. As our petanq yet more gentle. They play on grasse! It growes well – the rain doth make it soe.

Yet in thysse gentilitie there is constante talk of death. Even the children I hear makinge threats against theyr felowes. I heard todaie a child say, "I shall kill mie teachere" – she show'd no remorse. Death falls from her as naturallie as the rain from the skies. Bloodie Maria dids't burn some three hundred soules thirty years gone and the killinges end not – now twixt the 'good' Jesuits and those that favour the false queene. Drunkenesse is all around. Is it the hard life onlie?

I see fear in menne's eyes. A feare of which G-d to declare or which flag to follow. In some the distress can be smell'd. They drink in the tavernas all daie. Boldnesse leads to lust and I know it to be sated in these alleys wyth whores or in the hedgerowes wyth womenne who they have onlie recente met whils't drunk. Or they shall go to theyr beds and take theyr wyffes most violentlie. I drink to mie cups at home. I promise thee I shall not do the same here. If G-d wills it I shalle survive thysse great adventure. But feare shalle remayne and I shall not drinke until I am heal'd bie your love.

An old womanne cries out to sell the newes. She grippes sheets of papere wyth newes wrytte upon them. It is latin writ. She calls and stands. Daie after daie in rain and sunshine. I admire her strength. Her hair is lanke and grey. Her eyes caste down, her calling constante. Perhappes she hath lost here manne to the sea. Perhappes she has no manne. The tarres walk pass'd and she looks at them not. Occassionallie a rich manne stops to cast hysse gaze o'er the news and occasionallie he passeth her monnaie. She seems not to care. I shall speake wyth her. Perhappes I shalle be newes, "Spanniarte found in Dartmouth!" Perhappes not.

August iv

We are but a fewe hours from Dart castillo. A place call'd Totnesse. A most warringe town. They have a round fort, smallere than the defences at Lugo and not so high. It is atop a hill from whych it must be possible to see for manie miles.

The menne suggest'd we take a cart from the inn and I find myselffe searchinge for a brewe wytch. The customes here are barbaric. Brewe wytches are small tavernas where ale and birra are sold for less than the towne taverna prices. And they are persecuted most dreadfullie. If they are caught theyr tavernas are raz'd and the womenne burn't at the stake! A fowle habit. Wolf saies thysse is to prevent these women taking trade from the innkeepers (all menne). Yet there is no shortage of trade.

"These hills seem so far from the coast yet they hide much that can onlie be deville's work – the burninge, the killinge of womenne, the pressing of young boys to make tarres of them"

He is right. And indeed these hills are most fayre. Sheep graze, the hay is made. Small houses lie at peace as far as the eye can see. I know not why Felipe convinces himselffe that the Englishe are a daemon people. Perhappes he knows the fayte of brewe wytches! One of the menne at the Dartmouth taverna call'd London an aberration. If the people that dwell there are the same, then those that govern thysse fair country are daemons indeed.

We have walk'd to a small church wyth graves around. We sitte in thysse graveyard. One is mark'd "Marie Bosanquet, mothere of six, died thysse daie, ix maie, 1566." How many times did poore dead Marie fear for lyffe and the lyffe of her children as they came into thysse worlde? How manie times did she grieve the loss of a child that died at birth or later – from the pox, or the fever? Womenne bear so much pain in thysse lyffe and very little is of theyr owne makinge.

The daie is most stille. A fewe clouds. Sun-light shewes lines of ancient trees on the ridge. Oaks, I suspect. The menne sytte in the sun – Wolf, Padraig, Alonzo. A little tired from theyr revels but happie enough. Alonzo is eating grapes. Grapes! Where dids't he find them? He is growen gaunt. Hysse diet has not made him a soldier who can do much ere battle is join'd. We must leave thysse idyll and returne to our shippe.

auguste v

Nowe we have enter'd a new realm of madnesse. I

believe that Alonzo and Padraig have join'd Wolf in seeing our great adventure as noe more than the chance to visite Englishe tavernas and try theyr luck wyth wenches.

We sail'd to the gulf of the Solente thysse morning at the place the Englishe calle the Wight Isle. Immediately Wolf suggest'd we try our luck on shore. The tarres do not know how to respond to Wolf's commands – he hath a way of speakinge that would suggest an admirale or duke, not the son of a glovemaker. He demand'd a patacha, cast away from the *San Juan* and here we are – not two hour's rowing from her, the patache safely tied to the harbour wall, and us – in a taverna. Drinking, laughing, Wolf occasionallye suggesting we speake louder as, "There must be at least one person here who knowes not we are Spanniartes."

"And Eirish," saies Padraig.

"Portugaise alsoe," offers a barely hush'd Alonzo and I join in, "Gallegan, if it pleases you alle."

We are looked upon wyth little interest. Wolf's garb excites noe remark though I believe he has gone some way in attempting to encourage alle to gaze at him in awe. We are lucky the Englishe are less aware of fashion than the most backward Mollucanns. An Englishmanne sees guts extended bie beer as a great attraction to womenne. Alsoe, unless the manne be a playwrite when he must wear hose of the tightest virtue to appear attractive to actors, poets and other charlatans – as Padraig would'st have yt – he should covere an ill-fitting shirt wyth the night's dinner. Wolf looks for all the worlde like a bird of paradise by comparison.

Despite mie friend's apparelle, thysse is, in truth, a sowle-less place. It was, I thinke, drab and poore but hath been recent paint'd to seem newe. Onlie one wall is adorn'd. Yt is cover'd in writinge telling of vicyualles sold here. Some posters are here alsoe that disguise some letters. Thysse gives an effect most curious. "Visit the Gr..." follow'd by "panis" and "gustye...winde." "A kind of shelter....a tabernacle(!) to purchase the edibles of the worlde."

"Dark buttere from the Turke, aromatic teas from the Indies and Cathay" (no mentione here of Drake and hysse pirattes seizing alle on the trade routes of Portugale). And at the last, "breade and sweetmeats from the continent."

I think that we are thysse continent of whych these Englishe speake so free. The othere walls are a clean white that I have not seen before. There is a stage and some players arrive. The menne barely look up as they start theyr playinge – guitares and a cymbale. They are ignor'd by all. One calls to the assembl'd tarres to dance.

Wolf turns to me. "I cannot dance. It is a disappointment to mie wyffe." He looks asham'd. At last, I have found something mie friend admits he cannot do! Wolf saies, "These beggares are to be remark'd. A womanne ask'd me, wyth fowle breath and fewe teeth, for a little monnaie. She gav'est an exact amount and rambl'd about her need for bread. I gave her coin and she repeat'd, nay, demand'd the exact amount. I do believe she may really buy bread wyth yt."

The musicke moves us little tho Alonzo is tapping hysse fingers on the table and Padraig begins to sway. I tell Wolf of the dancing to our drums in the tavernas of Galicia. He knewe not of thysse tradition. Some menne here cast disapproving glances at the stage. The players have fix'd theyr smiles and are attempting loude clapping to give courage to the tarres. There are fewe womenne but they talk on, not looking to the musicke at all. There is no carousinge. None have tattoes but I see them hold the gaze of any tarre that look theyr way.

Perhappes theyr hath been trouble here of late – the inn-keeper and hysse wenches keep constante watch. For feare a fight will start? I see none who might be so inclin'd. The musicke doth drone on and I attempt to write as Wolf advises.

What do I feele? Thysse is hard indeed. The noyse and the false cheer from the stage take mie feelings from me. Soe I stare at mie birra and praie for peace so at least some thought shall come. Wolf hath said that thysse is mistak'n. Thinkinge doth not make writinges happen. Words may be in mie mouth and thoughts in mie sowle but writinge is in mie fingeres and hands as planting is in the hands of those that tend the soyle.

As the menne talk on around me I feel a slight release as Wolf suggests and words appear on the page. Mie fingeres talk as they talk on your body as we make love. I write as mie tongue licks your sexe – as a manne possess'd. I falter again – no words flow. I see Wolf hath taken up hysse quille and begins to scribble – trulye a writer, and lover – but not a dansere. Ha! He goes nowe to the inne-keeper and demands ale. He raises a tankard and I am summons'd to hysse side. The band play on. I disregard them and at last words come. As some eyes are turn'd to mie good looking friend I turn to the clean wall, and wyth no small guilty pleasure, I place a mark upon yt – a Morganne Davidde! It is a start.

Words followe – O travellere, stay thy wearie feet – drinke of thysse fountain pure and sweete – yt flowes for rich and poore the same. Now I am a poet, though a poore one. I trust yt might bring some comfort to othere menne bor'd bie the attempt'd revels of bands such as these – if the land-lorde doth not paint yt o'er wyth white when he sees yt. Whosoever reads yt shall not know yt was writ bie a love-lorn jewe serving Felipe's great cause.

A beggare assails me. Unkemp't he rambles. Calles me "friend". The land-lorde is quicke and tumbles thysse newe friend from hysse place on the instante. As he did so, he glanc'd at mie scribbl'd poetry. I doubt mie scrawl shalle last the night. I shall rest mie head here and sleep a while.

I am wak'd. By songe. Wolf and Alonzo wyth two or three otheres sing most bawdilie:

Westron winde, when will thou blow,
The smalle raine downe can raine?
Crist, if my love wer in my armis
And I in my bed againe.

Who shall have my faire lady?
Who shall have my faire lady?
Who but I, who but I, who but I?
Under the levis grene!

How can they know the wordes so soon. I slumbere agayne. And wake to more!

The fairest man
The best love can
Dandirly, dandirly,
Dandirly, dan
Under the levis grene.

Dandirly indeede. A pretty dittie. More sleep takes me.

Wolf nowe stands before me. I am bleারie. He is bloodie'd. He hath been struck about the head and face. "I should learn to speake mie mind less," quoth he. He was watching o'er me (whils't drinking and singing) and he saies to Padraig, "That manne is too fat to live!" He saies that he had intend'd a simple comment but yt was o'er-heard and taken as a threat. The manne was asleep but Wolf's remark was heard by hysse companions. A rough fellow lumber'd to mie friend and demand'd he repeat hysse words. Wolf is capable of dangerous calme at such momentes. "That manne is too fat to live," he said again, smiling.

"Are you looking for trouble?" bellow'd the tarre and all went quiet.

"I have troubles enough," Wolf replied, "but what ails thee, friend." Wolf's newe friend lash'd out wyth hysse fists and all hell was loos'd, Wolf and Padraig doing theyr best against three or four tarres in theyr cups. Yt is a wonder any blows found theyr mark but Wolf seems to have put hysse face in the way at least twice. Padraig escap'd lightly. Wolf saies at one point Padraig pull'd a table back and call'd for more ale so he might enjoy the skirmishe. Alonzo sat back and gave odds on who might win!

All was soon calme again. Wolf's brutish friend return'd to hysse drinking and I was woken by my bloodie'd companion. We shalle soon go to our beds.

I thinke Wolf is too rous'd to sleep much. Thysse shall be regard'd as "a good night out" by the Englishe!

A womanne enters, her hair clasp'd back on her

head. A beauteous face. Yet she wears boots! Black like her jerkin and hose. The tarres part as she passes and avert theyr gaze. She walks to one of the whores and they speake soft before the whore smiles and leads her outside to the alleye.

August vi

We are return'd to the *San Juan* and heare of an attack. The *Gran Grifon* fell astern last night and was set upon by the Englishe. Yt sounds an uneven battle – the *Revenge* and two galleones pitt'd against an urca manned by many alreadie sicke. Sixty or more are injured and she was onlie saved by Recalde scouting west.

The mood is sombre. Thysse adventure turns to true warre. I thinke we have but seen skirmishes until nowe. We are in formation again and can see the Englishe coast to our port-side. We shall head soon for our rendezvous wyth Parma. Alonzo wagers he shalle not be there! If soe then our journie is wasted. He hath promis'd Felipe troops to help wyth an invashunne of the sun-filled lands that we see to the leeward.

Our progress is steady, the Englishe always to

our rear. The weather is kind. If I were a gull I could look down upon the fleet and see a great crescent heading for the Ffrench coast. Padraig thinks we must make landfall at Dunkirk or Nieuport. Wolf hears rumour that the sand-banks on thysse shore are traitorous – lying too shallow to take our keel – and we have no local pilots who can guide us through in safety.

sonndaie

It must be close to midnight. We hear that Parma has not come and wait in some trepidation. Wolf thinkes we are in crescent formation stille. The *San Juan* lies close to the *San Martin*. We are at anchore and it is quiet.

Ffireshippes! How can thysse be? From peace and nought but the sound of menne talking and gentle waves to great cries that rend the night air. There must be ten or more burning shippes bearinge down on our fleet. They approach'd most quiet then one explod'd in the night – from dark hulk to blazing star in a moment. The tarres know what these shippes can do. Theyr timberes are pitch'd and pour forth smoke and flames.

One explodes! "The bastards fill them wyth gun-powdere", cries Padraig. We are ordered below decks but fewe obey. The tarres attempt to lift anchor and do not haul fast enough. Two menne are call'd aft to hack at the rope wyth cutlasses. The hawser is fast cut and I feel neath mie feet the *San Juan* heel leeward on the tide.

Two adventuros stand nowe on the foredeck and shout to the Englishe to fight like menne. "Cowards! Hide behind fire and smoke but we shall have thee!" Brave words but I see feare in these menne alsoe. The Englishe are noe fools. They are somewhere beyond the smoke.

"They wait for us to clear the baie in panicke," sayeth Wolf. Some menne are franticke wyth feare. The *San Martin* is ring'd close bie our galleones but our admirale hath set pinnaces at the fireshippes.

"They are grappling wyth them", Wolf saies quietly and he is right. I can see some of our menne drawinge close to a fireshippe nowe. They throw a rope aboard and I see a manne scalinge it to her deck. Thysse is beyond reason. One manne against a burning barque!

"He returnes," a manne cries and we see our brave tarre dive to the waters. "The fireshippes are on set course nowe," saies Alonzo. We can but flee. Alle is noyse, smoke and flame. The *San Martin* is turning about and striking a course through the burning shippes.

"He heads for the *Hinde*," a crie goes up. "Nowe shalle we see how these Englishe can fight." "He intends to smite Grenville," sayeth Wolf, almost too quiet to hear. The *Hinde* shewes no sign of panicke. There are menne who steady themselffes wyth musket as our admirale approaches.

The *San Martin* is nowe under full sail and heads straight for Grenville's glorie. These are menne to be reckon'd wyth. We thought an armada shippe in full sail to be a thing of terrible beauty and had, I thinke, imagin'd that all would turn and flee before us. But not the *Hinde*. Nor others that come to her aide.

It is but momentes ere the *San Martin* set upon her course and alreadie she rakes the *Hinde* wyth cannon fire. "She hath pass'd." cries Alonzo. And he is right. As our flag-shippe sails onward she is quicke pursued bie others intent upon her destruction.

monndaie

The *San Lorenzo* is crippl'd! I see her rowinge to the leeward heading for Calaise. Her red sails are clear to us. All who manne the oars are convict'd menne, alsoe dress'd in red. Thysse lucky coloure shalle not help them nowe. They row for theyr very lives – and freedom?

The *Arke* hath turn'd to give chase. These shippes are slow but can still move fastere than our galleases and galleones. There is no mercy in thysse Englishe admirale – and little courage. Why is he not to windward defending hysse countrie from our fleet? It is surely treasure he seeks. May G-d save us!

The *San Lorenzo* has run aground. She falters and now heels landward. I see ropes and halyards swinging from her yards and mightie waves sent skyward as she heels o'er. Alreadie she lies as if beach'd, her seaboard cannones aim onlie to the sky and are no defence agains't the *Arke*. The sea cannot be deep enough for the *Arke* to assail her further. Can the menne escape to the shore?

Wolfe grasps me and points to the strick'n shippe. The menne around are shouting and mighty distress'd. They shake theyr fists and curses fly from theyr lips as I watch longboats fill'd wyth musketeers strike out for the *San Lorenzo*. Both sides let loose shot and manie fall.

A manne in the first longboat takes a gut-shot, blood coveres hysse fellowes in an instant and he falls back. Anothere is shot twixt the shoulders and he spins around. He falls against anothere who quicke pushes him o'erboard. The sea is alreadie red wyth blood and the foam washes pink and crimson, not white.

The smoke from the muskets is not yet thicke but manie menne are hit as they wade for the shore. "Thysse is murder," saies Wolf as two more of our menne fall .....

All goes quiet. The muskets have ceas'd. Wolfe saies thysse must mean a captain's death. "Not de Moncado" he wagers. "The good Don will have made hysse escape afore now." The menne are abandoning the *Lorenzo*. Is Don Hugo slain? The Englishe clamber o'er her side as a swarm of locustes.

"Ravening dogs," cries Alonzo. The Englishe will loot the ground'd *Lorenzo*. We can do nothing. T'is too shallow to approach and too far to have success wyth musket tho menne still fire occasionallye.

Nowe utter confusion – the French fire on the Englishe from the port. Are they turn'd now to our side?" "Where is Parma?" screams a manne and the crie is echo'ed throughout the *San Juan*.

The battle – for battle thysse is – is properlie join'd. We can see Drake himselffe approaching the *San Martin*! They are perilous close and cannone shot is fired, the *Revenge* first. She is well named. For what ill Drake seeks revenge I know notte.

"Look nowe" cries Wolf. More of Drake's squadron surround the Duke. These Englishe are too fleet for us. The *Swallow* and *Victory* are there.

Now Oquendo approaches in the bless'd *Santa Ana*, nowe the *San Mateo* heaves into view. We join close as Don Diego would have it and all is abandon'd chaos. Wood splinters all around as shot finds its mark. A manne writhes wyth spinters through hysse forearm, blood spurts from hysse thigh and he falls forward wyth such a pleadinge look in hysse eyes... We fire in vain as Drake passes.

Alonzo gestures and I see more Englishe. "The *Vanguard*," mutters Wolf. There will soon be fifteen of us – the Englishe shall do well to challenge our muster. Soon all the galleones will protect the Duke.

"Do not speake too quicke," saies Wolf as we are struck by cannone and musket shotte. I may die here (where do such thoughts come from?) – on a cold night wythin sight of a countrie I have ne'er seen, for a king who I shall n'er understand.

Alonzo returns from the crow's nest (he hath the limbs of a monkey). He has seen the *Felipe* surround'd. She is shot beyond measure, her foremast sunder'd and her rudder torn. Death hangs o'er her as smoke billowes from below decke. The *San Mateo* was heading to her aide but Alonzo feares she too is shotte to a halte.

He thinkes he saw an English tarre leap aboard – there are menne, madmenne and Englishmenne. Sidonia is in theyr mids't and may yet save them tho hysse *San Martin* is grevious shot. Our menne fight now onlie wyth arquebusses. There is no defence against the faster shippes of Frobisher and Howard.

A lull. The Englishe are demandinge that Toledo surrenders the *San Felipe*. He is surround'd. We do not help tho hysse plight is all too clear. We are too far behind and may soon be in the midst of the Englishe galleones. Two men fall, hit at the same time. Blood and theyr guts now drench our foredeck, menne groan or lie stille, theyr skinne alreadie a pallour most deathlie. A man screams and holds a torn arm. Blood soakes hysse shirt. Wolf goes to him but the manne pushes him away and is hit again immediate. Hysse forehead bursts as a shot takes him from behind. He spins and Wolf moves to the side to let him fall, hysse brains coursing from hysse skulle.

Another walks toward us wyth fear in hysse eyes, a leg torn by shot. He drags himselffe toward the door to the galley. Flames arch from the doorway and screams follow. Despair is all around.

A crie is made that the *San Felipe* sinketh. She has turn'd to the coast, the *San Mateo* alsoe adrift. There must be alreadie hundreds drown'd and it is not yet nightfall. The *Maria Juan* is desperate alsoe. The crewe are in her rigginge – she hath no rudder nor mizzen. Boats are cast to her aide – I feare she is to be taken by the sea.

Auguste viij

Such memories. We have sail'd north following Sidonia. The battle is before mie eyes as I write though it is two daies since we made our escape. I give pause and am hand'd a pipe bie Wolf in silence. I accep't a flame from Wolf and the smoke calmes me. It clouds and clears mie perceivinge at the same time.

Mie bodie needs reste and the tobaccoe gives it that appearance but the vision of the *San Martin* pursued is nowe more clear. As the Englishe galleones gave chase I could see Sidonia's's tarres fore and afte setting sail and hauling on rope for deare lyffe. As we watch'd another galleone appeared from the north but five leagues from her quarrie. Drake in the *Revenge.* To be pursued bie such as Grenville was poore luck enough but to be fac'd bie Drake!

Bearing down as an eagle upon her prey the Englishe did not fire until the last moment. I saw the *San Martin*'s forward cannone fire as she tried to put about. I know not what the duke was thinkinge – to face three galleons rather than Drake? As she turn'd she rak'd Drake's shippe wyth shot. But Drake let loose such a volley!

Wolf sayeth that one cannon ball pass'd clean through the *San Martin.* What horror thysse must have seem'd below decke. I saw the *Revenge* struck four or more times bie our fire. The

Englishe tarres would have been lacerat'd bie splinteres, more torn bye theyr owne vessel's shatter'd timbers than any stray musket shot.

They were given no time to fear fire from the powder kegs stor'd below for alle attention was turn'd to an Englishe calamitie of theyr owne making. Two of the galleons following the *San Martin* tangl'd spars. We had been distract'd bie the *Revenge* and perhappes her advance had misled the captains of the shippes wyth the *Hinde.*

A great commotion and confusion seem'd to follow. One shippe was the strongere and pitch'd the other to leeward. As she did soe we saw Sidonia attempt to turn again. And now the *Revenge* herselffe was taken bie surprise. Turning against the tide the *San Martin* plowed through the waves making mighty spume and spray. Heading north east she slowe pull'd away from Grenville and Sidonia raised the signal for retreat.

Was thysse the end of our adventure? To have fought for less than two daies not far from the French coast but still a daie's sailing from any hope of reaching Marrgate as plann'd.

Our own plight was lessen'd bie these events. Aramburu is not a manne to be so easily distract'd and as tarres seem'd to flie amongst the rigging setting sail, so we head'd after our flagshippe. Below deck were sights to bring tears and pity to the most prideful adventuro or king. Menne shot to pieces, blood swilling cross the boards, a manne wyth no arm and anothere wyth both legs shot away. I breathe deep on mie pipe and mie vision clears.

There remayneth nought butte the *San Martin* and ten more vessels some way from her, alle our owne. In these last two daies the Englishe appear content to follow. We can see the *Hinde* and the *Hope*. The *Revenge* cannot be far behind. They do not attack us. Perhappes they know we have nowhere but the cold north to go. We feel escort'd from theyr shores as a landlord might escort a drunken reveller lest he perform some mischief.

Padraig saies the Englishe need not fear us. He hath not seen any of our shot do harm to theyr shippes. Yt seems to fall short or break against theyr hulls.

"Yt is not the fault of our gunneres, nor the cannones. These are well made, some caste in Englande! But the shot is poore, caste in Portugale and quench'd too soon. Yt is weaken'd and brittle. We have sail'd hundreds of leagues to fire cake at Grenville and Drake!"

August ix

More of the armada joins us. We are in crescent forme once more. Padraig thinks thysse shall be a terrible journie. We must go north. There is no turning nowe against the Englishe. The wind is to the south west and drives us on. Alonzo thinks onlie a miracle can save us – and the Englishe have more than theyr share of G-d's deliverance.

Yet miracle thysse newe wind may yet be. Yt will take us far to the north and bring us closer to Hibernia, a countrie still in sympathie wyth Spain. If we do not make landfall there we shall have over seven hundred leagues to travel. Seven hundred! Wyth menne dying from wounds and thirst, the food ranke. Thysse will test us all, in body and spirite.

Yt is three weeks since we left Corunna and we may be at sea at least a month more. We shall surely die from lack of agua?

August xi

De Cuellar is call'd to the *Lavia*. We were makinge good headway, a good south-westerlie wind and the Englishe in pursuit. Sidonia had fir'd a signale for us to make short saile so Ricalde and hysse shippes might reach us. But two of our number, Wolf saies the urca *Santa Barbara* and a galleone, the *San Pedro*, did not shorten sail. The captaine of the *San Pedro* is one Francisco de Cuellar. Hysse shippe mov'd ahead of the fleet, even beyond Sidonia – yt is claim'd he slept.

Some of us have been call'd to hysse trial heard by de Aranda on *La Lavia* – I know not why Wolf and I were chosen, I suspect Wolf barter'd for thysse new adventure. He was mightie sicke of pumping belowe deck – Padraig saies the caulking is sore test'd by these seas. She spewes her oakum and there are great gaps in her timbers where the ingot's are loos'd.

De Aranda has heard the pleas of Don Cristobal de Avila, captaine of the *Santa Barbara* and no clementcy offer'd. He is to be hung and hysse body shewe'd to the rest. Nowe De Cueller faces the Advocate. He stands accus'd by Bovadillo. Bovadillo must surely be asham'd that we are in flight. Hysse soldiers have had no chance to fight – unless you count the musketrie they display'd as we fled the ffireshippes.

De Cuellar is an impassion'd man. Hysse pleas

are pitiful, yet honest. He pleads that he hath perform'd hysse duty beyond hysse callinge and if he speakes false, he would willingly be cut to pieces by hysse own menne. I fear Bovadillo shall not respect the truth of thysse manne. He shewed noe remorse in quicke condeming de Avila.

All is quiet. We can see the Englishe far astern. They must finde thysse interlude most confusing. Some of the tarres will not look at De Cuellar. They know he is a brave and loyal captain. There has been noe sign of Recalde and Sidonia. They leave de Cuellar's fayte in the hands of a bitter and dangerous man. The sentence is pass'd. The word spreads as fire through the shippe. De Cuellar shall lose hysse command and remayne on the *Lavia*! Perhappes even dogs of warre such as Bovadillo have mercie in them.

Wolf is subdued. "Let's go," he sayeth wyth sadness in hysse eyes and we leave de Cuella to hysse newe master.

Aboard the *San Juan* we are issu'd wyth newe orders. We are to hold a newe bearing of North North East until we find 61 degrees. We must then run West South West until 58 degrees and then South East bound for Finestra! We are to avoid Irrellanda as there are warreing folk there and we have no mappe of that coast. “Warreing! Warreing!” cries Padraig. “To be sure you shalle miss the land of peace and plenty.”

August xij

I have seen much that might make a man despondent, even unto wishing hysse lyffe end’th. Manie deaths, injuries too terrible to be relat’d, sicknesse, the terror of menne who know’st they shalle die before home is reach’d.

But nowe, as I write, I see something that makes the heart lift, a sight more welcome than the calme sea that came on us thysse morning and wyth more room for laughter than the strongest jests and japes I have yet encounter’d. Padraig, Alonzo and Wolf ...... are playing petanq! The menne stand and cheer, Aramburu himselffe stands at the poop all smiles, distract’d from hysse constant concern that we are follow’d. Some of the sicke are here – Alonzo takes wagers in between casting hysse boule.

Thysse morning Wolf came to Padraig and they whisper’d some. They went o’er to Alonzo and all three crep’t out, glancing around and Wolf touching hysse finger to hysse lips to signify I should be silent. They were gone a fewe moments and returned – wyth shotte! Wolf held three balls from an esmeril and Padraig three more. I could not see what Alonzo had clasp'd in hysse hand. He reveal'd a ball from hysse arqubusse! Wolf signall'd I should follow and the foure of us went on deck.

The swell was subdue'd todaie and the shippe sail'd smoothe through sea so frequentlye turbulent, nowe in disguise as a quiet lake. We clear'd space on decke – movinge hawsers and rope and a fewe baskets – and then began our game. The first time Alonzo hurl'd hysse small shot, a half dozen menne came forward in surprise. The first time Wolf hurl'd hysse cannon shott (and split the deck) Aramburu himselffe stepp'd forward.

All was quiet. A hush descend'd on the menne and Aramburu took in the scene. Wolf wink'd at Padraig and another shot flew through the air. It struck the arquebusse ball – and a cheer went up. Aramburu grinn'd, nodd'd to Wolf and the sport had begun!

Wolf and Padraig playe a fine game. On occasion Wolf throws hysse boule high into the air and yt crashes to the deck. Yt hath twice gone through! Some poor sowle will be disturb'd from hysse sick-bedde. We are in danger of killinge more wyth our own shotte than the Englishe manag'd thysse last fewe daies.

Nowe Padraig stands clear and he and Wolf are in whisper'd talk. Alonzo joins them and I see hysse features blush. I walk to mie friends. "I don't believe yt," Padraig is saying. "Red and gold?"

"And the haire on her head as dark as the soyle," replies Wolf. They are discussing – I blushe to write thysse – quinnies! Alonzo is transfix'd as Wolf and Padraig suspend theyr game – to whisper of the quinnies they have knowen. Wolf saies that he knew a womanne in Girona who had dyed her pubis the coloures of Spain. Wyth henna and limone she had the made the most beauteous mound – a deep red and gold – "Like the sun," saies Wolf. I wonder what more Alonzo might learn if we are able to sytte once more in a taverna!

August xvi

Padraig must die. He hath lain in hysse birth since we came across the Englishe galleone. Such terrible fortune – alreadie hundreds of leagues to the north of battle, free of all threat but the weather and the long journie home. Then the galleone appear'd to leeward. Noe warning, just a swift approach and broadside and she had gone – leaving a great hole in our side and splinters and shards in our dear friend.

Hysse body is pierc'd through and through and none can see how he might survive. There was much blood at first, the berthe awash wyth Padraig's and that of other poor sowles. He hath been dry these last fewe hours and is colde to the touch. He raves quietlie and sings occasionallye. A Gallic song, perhappes a lullabye. Hysse eyes see nothing. Hysse hand grippes mie wrist as a manne might hold to a rope for dear lyffe and feare of the fall. Hysse skinne is sallowe though I cannot believe the lyffe is ready to leave him.

Our surgeone extract'd two great shards from hysse leg and hysse left arm hangs limp. He shall not hold hysse love again wyth that arm. He has a grievous wound to hysse head. Wolf sittes wyth us, quiet and doleful. He writes nothing. I see hysse despair where once I saw onlie laughter and a lust for lyffe. I know he hath lost friends before – to battle, to the cancre - but to lose Padraig nowe –

after soe much triumph and suffering together – is hard indeed. He leans close as Padraig sings. I believe he attempts the Gallic phrases. Hysse lips move in time wyth Padraig's and our berthe is took sudden wyth the soft sound of a children's song. A song to bring us all sleep. Other menne take up the refrayne as I listen. To mie shame I crie a little. Wolf looks up and – amids't such sadness and death – he smiles. A smile of lyffe, of comfort, of solidaritie. I sing. We have a gentle trio, three menne join'd by suffering – and love.

Padraig sings noe more. Hysse sowle hath flowen. Wolf leans forward and takes our friend in hysse arms. Our tears are not manlie. I praie Padraig is wyth hysse mother. Hysse song call'd for her and a remembrance of hysse child-hood. We haul hysse broken body to the decke and wrap him in Wolf's costlie jerkin. No longer does Wolf care for such extravagance.

Padraig is caste to the sea. Felipe's army of sowles is divid'd twixt those that live and those that await theyr companions in gehenna.

The shippe heaves. Wolf watches the sea take our friend and turns to me, no longer asham'd of hysse tears. We know Padraig is safe. No further harm can come to him. Yt is our grieffe that lives on, not hysse owne. Perhappes he will return as fysshe or fowle to journie wyth us until it is our turn to join him again. Wolf shivers and comes forward. We embrace.

August xx

A shippe is lost! We woke thysse morninge in the rough'st sea. So manie sicke and in agony from wounds and the torment of the waves. Then a crie went up that the *Castillo Negro* had blowen off course.

There is no sign. The waves remayne mountainous and the rollinge most vexaccious, yet we had stay'd in rough formation until we spied a most lonelie rock. As we tack't to south the *Castillo* was torn from our view and pitch'd to leeward. Wythin moments she could'st no longere be seen. I feare for her menne and praie G-d she will continue not across the great ocean. There is nought there but Bysse. Wolf saies Bysse is mere invention – an imagininge of former navigateurs that is yet mark'd on manie charts.

Thysse writinge is now, ytselffe, a form of madnesse. As I scrawl the inke slides before the aim of my quille. If you e'er read thysse yt shalle be onlie with my aid as I guide you through the spillinges cross the page. Wolf stays mie hand and saies I should beware lest mie words of hope (to be wyth you) be translat'd by G-d into the wreckinge of our vessel.

I have been on deck but brieflie. Alle is awash. The tarres hold to theyr ropes lash'd bie wind and rain but haul on command. We have no saile. The wind would surelie take it wyth our masts. Grey clouds cover the skies from horizon to horizon and a storm builds the like of wych I have never seen. A daie's rain of thysse kind would feed our streams and springs for a full yeare in the cordillara or the picos.

At least there is no sign of our enemie. We have travell'd for daies with onlie our fellowes as company Now one is lost.

August xxij, 1588

O mie fayre love, how can I tell of thysse? Dear Alonzo is in agonie. For two daies we have seen horses and burros swimminge in desparation as we pass amongst them. They have been throwinge the poore beasts to the waters to make the shippes less burden'd. Some drowne quicke. Otheres swim on wyth much feare (and truste?) in theyr eyes. Thysse morninge we were told to throw our own poore beasts o'er. Wolfe sayeth it would surely be better to eat them as we nowe onlie have biscuit – and agua, from rain. Some have wine and I thinke yt quencheth them not. Wolf was ignored and the horses and burros are throwen to the waves.

Alonzo was ask'd to lead hysse sad companion to her end and he at first refused. He clung to her neck as a child might to hysse mothere. Two tarres pull'd him away and he let out grevious wails as hysse marre was heav'd across decke, hoist'd aft and throwen o'erboard. She thrashes stille in the waves wyth otheres of her cavalrie. I can see ten or more pitiful beasts swimming on behind the San Juan.

Alonzo struggles less. I feel hysse spirit is forlorne. Hysse will is broken. He cannot look to the waters. Laduenda swims on, steady nowe. Her eyes are less fearfull and she is a fine horse. There is no land – she must drowne. Some of the beasts are pitiful thynne. They have little lyffe left in them and fall behind quicke or slip 'neath the waves. Yet Laduenda still moves in steady fashion awaitinge her mastere. She keeps her eyes on Alonzo. Not pleadinge as a lover might. A simple trustinge.

The menne let Alonzo go. He hath ceas'd hysse struggles and walked aft. I start toward him but Wolf stays mie arm. "Let him go to her." I am sore perplex'd. Can he mean.... Alonzo turns to us. He smiles and hysse laughinge mouth opens wide in the wind. I hear him not. He raises a hand, turns again – and leaps!

Menne, Wolf and I alsoe, rush to the side. Alonzo is in the waves, swimming toward Laduenda. Around him are burros and one or two cavalrie horse. They swim on and he ignores them as does hysse mare. They are join'd. He takes her mane and nowe the two of them swim together. Menne call to him and beg the captain to turn about. It is not possible in such a tide. Slowly we make our course west. Alonzo and Laduenda fall behind.

"Tis a fine death", saies Wolf, hysse eyes far away, thinking of our own deaths to come? "At least Alonzo has chosen to die wyth one he loves." I aske G-d for little but I praie he dies contente.

september i

Thysse journie shalle kill me. I shalle not die of the fever or flux, nor shall I starve – the derid'd baccallou remaynes for any still able to eat. Manie are too sicke or already dead soe there is food of a kind for Wolf, myselffe and otheres that yet live – I thinke about two hundred sowles onlie. I shall die of mie lonelinesse for you. I have not knowen such losse.

Menne speake less nowe of Spain. When they speake at all yt is to praie for the pitchinge to cease and the tide to carry us south again. I thinke onlie of you. Wolf speakes little. He too is a lost sowle. He stares aft again and again for the miracle of Alonzo's return. He praies I thinke and at night gazes at the aurora to the north.

When I venture on decke wyth him I look onlie south. I thinke of you safe at the house of your fathere, sleeping quiet wyth your bellye growing round, fill'd wyth our sonne. You will wake and go to your toilette, you will carry agua to wash. I shall wake sudden, still standing on the boards, mie limbs sore wyth fatigue and the stench of sickeness from below. I know not if mie owne sickness then is the flux or the wrenching emptiness of missing your touch. Your smile, your haire, your sweet breath, laughtere and sexe. Even nowe I can feel you press'd against me. Thysse is delirium. All that presses is the side of the *San Juan* as she rolls in the sea. She knoweth not the way home herselffe but must be guid'd by those that are lost.

We are met wyth Calderon in the *San Sebastien.* He hath secret'd rice and other foods in her hold. Aramburu has paid a princely sum for thysse treasure. Yt moves Wolf not at alle.

September v

We head west. All is turmoil. The waves are mountainous. Woulds't that we might find the wall that is spoken of by Cosmas butt we sail on, wyth no hope of end, nor sight of land.

Menne are sicke all around as we manne the pumps. The shippe spews her oakum and the sea comes through gaping holes in the hull all the time. None have dry clothes. Most are too weak to help us in our labours. I know notte how manie are dead. Even as I write a manne twists in hysse death agonie while a fewe of us pump the water around hysse bunk. The water is ranke, the stench nowe one of death as much as rott'd food. There are vermin all o'er the shippe. We ignore them. Some try to drink wine, others take theyr own pisse for what little relief yt brings.

Even if, by G-d's favour, we reach Corunna or Rivero I am sure we shall be too weak to guide the *San Juan* safely to harbour.

But thysse is an idle fancy. I doubt we shall see out thysse very night. We are lost. Yt is too dark-cloud'd to use the starres as a guide and we have not seen the sun these three daies. On occasione a crie goes up that a shippe is seen but yt is always too far and we onlie catch a brieffe glimpse – of a mast, or a sail. I know not how manie shippes are blowen in thysse great ocean. Wolf saies there may be close to a hundred but the barques and urcas have no chance in these seas.

Sept ix, 1588

We are lost. Yt is soe colde. There has been a freezinge myste for five daies. We see nothinge of our companions. Wolf has been on decke and saies he can barelie see hysse owne hand. Two or three die dailie – I think of the colde. They eat soe little and the food is rott'd so we have onlie rain watere and the baccalou. It cannot give sustenance to menne weaken'd bie the flux.

Wolf saies there is noe sign of horizon or starres and knows notte how we are guid'd. Yt is too hard to pump. The sea breaks through our caulking more quicke than we can make rid of yt. We are bless'd with a calm race that makes the journie less tempestuous.

Sept xi, 1588

La Rata hath founder'd. The menne saie it is G-d's will that two tower'd shippes fail thus. They are not stable, the barques less so. The toweres are for infantriemenne, archers and musketeeres. Mie morisco friends did declare even in Lisboa that such shippes were the work of the deville – commission'd bie a kinge (Felipe) in G-d's name but on an errande of death – for gold and Felipe's glorie.

The first of *La Rata*'s toweres explod'd, as had *San Salvadore* off Plymmouth. I know not what caus'd it – a careless fuse in the powder store? As menne fell from the towere a mast fell o'er the forecastle and she alsoe was crush'd. I saw menne leap (to theyr deaths?) rathere than face the flames. One poor sowle was ablaze. Alreadie some claim that moriscoes or jewes set a powdere keg aflame. None may heare (nor speake) a fear'd truth - that the Invincible Armada is no longer invincible and thysse be the mission, not of G-d, but of a prideful king. So manie menne of good heart have gone to theyr deaths for a king they would never see and a G-d they fear'd hath desert'd them. For gold that they could but imagine and lands they would never even touch. Felipe praies for us? I thinke Felipe hath forgotten us as rich menne forget all but the desire for gold.

september xiij

When I sat in the taverna in Vigo I thought onlie of losinge you for a brief time and the chance of an adventure. I was fill'd wyth a kind of omnipotencie – a profound feelinge that the worlde was there for mie masterie, delights would come to me at little cost. I truly believ'd that to travel thousands of leagues amidst soldier and tarre, to face the waves, to fight for Felipe and more would be but an adventure – a diversion from the lyffe of the picos and minifundias of mie childhoode. I was arrogant and mistook. I have seen something of what the world can do to menne – the seas, the tides, the terrible storms, and more of what menne do to each othere. Now I write as a manne who knows not what to do in thysse worlde as the light seems to have died.

Wolf is dead! There is no sorrowe like thysse in a poor farmer's lyffe. At home I have lost a fewe friends though none that I consider part of mie sowle. No pain of partinge to compare. Since we embarqued I have lost mie countrie, mie home, mie love (I praie notte) and two dear ffreinds (Padraig and Alonzo) who shewed how it was possible in all thysse madnesse to fynde humour and companionshippe – even how to offere love wythout condition to a horse. But nowe the sky is dark, the rain never-endinge and I cannot begin to imagine that dawn shalle break – and I am furious that it shalle offere its glorie despite the death of mie greatest ffreind. I sytte and trie to write how Wolf shewed me. From the heart. Wythout censoringe mie lines. Nothing comes. Alle is black, the wordes have noe meaning. He is no longere here to offer a critic's comment.

Last eve he seemed quiet (for him). We were standing off the coast when a crie went up that an Eirishe boy had been caught. *La Lavia*, the *Juliana* and anothere had gone before us into the baie and, as we watch'd, a manne dived to the watere from the *Juliana*. He took but a fewe strokes and then lash'd out at some small thing in the waves. Thysse he carrie'd back to hysse vessel. A patache was sent o'er at Aramburu's command and the struggling bundle of rags brought back to the San Juan. It was a boy. No more than a childe.

Wolf went to him. I could see he brought memories of Padraig to mie friend. Wolf calmed him then indicated the baie. The boy sayeth, "Streedagh". Its name I suppose. Wolf looked most thoughtful and came to me. A little jestinge, some talke of our returne. Then he took me to one side. "What are we to do? Is there a purpose to lyffe beyond companionshippe and love Isidore? And what if that love fails thee or companionshippe prevents not the death of ffreinds? Do not look so sad dear Isidore, your friend is but in hysse cups again."

He took hysse ring from hysse fingere and gave yt to me. Wyth that he walk'd to the foredecke and watch'd a long time the starres. Starres he lov'd. It was a custom of hysse to compare hysse loves to the love of starres. A womanne could be worth ten starres, a childe five, Girona seven, a good drinke three. He once said that our ffreindshippe would come close to perfect in the writinges of a poet and might be as much as nine starres. As we left Hibernia we saw the great lights of the northern skies and he stood as a childe might, enraptur'd. On the foredecke he stood and star'd at the waters deep in thought. Was he remembering Lisboa, the sierra de guadarrama as he left Girona, the Escorial? Or later times. The times of companionshippe and love? The taverna in Dartmouth, the gunner's wyffe on the beach, the womenne at inn after inn?

He turn'd to me and beckon'd. "I have none to bid adieu to here butte you Isidore. I have seen enough nowe. I am tired. I have whor'd. I have drunk to mie cups. I have been honour'd to stand bie your side as a midwyffe. Alonzo's death was too much. A manne who could die for the love of a horse shames us alle. Thysse adventure ends nowe for me. I have oft thought of death but always at the hand of anothere – a fight o'er a womanne, a brawl in an inn, even a stray shot from somme Englishe musket. Now I understand that such deaths are not our own end but ends determin'd bie otheres. If they be G-d's will then G-d hath will'd it that we die at random or bie unseen enemie or misfortune. Is thysse the way a manne should die? By luck and happenstance alone? I cannot bear the weight in mie heart that thysse terrible adventure brings soe I aske you to witness mie last journie." He kiss'd me, turn'd, and dived to the waters.

I had thought thysse was one more jest. Onlie if death ytselffe is a comedie can I laugh nowe. Speechlesse I stood gazing to the water, trying in desparation to o'ercome the temptation to join him (forgive me). It was too late for ought but shock'd sorrow. No fanfare. None that knew or cared that mie friend had gone. A dark fortress sending one more death into the night. I could see nothing. No sign of ought but the waves against the hull.

Did hysse lonelie sowle slip neath the waves to hysse final rest? Soe simple a death. So utterlie at odds wyth hysse lyffe and love of it. It must be that he intend'd to swim to Streedagh though I heard no sound beyond the waters at our hull. I gazed on the ring. Inside an inscription: No tengo mas que dar te – I have nothinge more to give thee.

How can I go on?

september xv

San Juan de Portugal beats leeward from the Bleskies. Mie head and heart are fill'd wyth sorrowe for Wolfe. All seems lost. Twice in the night I found myselffe calling out to him. Fewe menne notic'd. Indeed there are fewe to notice ought. Wolf is just anothere manne gone missinge to them. And one of how manie? Three hundred? Four? Those that remain are in the poorest health.

It is too rank to go below decke at all nowe. Mie grieffe saw me fall twice. But fallinge is nothing here. And what would befall me if a tarre was to see mie plight? There are too manie deaths nowe for anything but the briefest mark of sorrow. I look around and understand that manie must share thysse grieffe though they speake of it not. Alle have lost companions, some surelie as dear as Wolf to me.

Two menne saw theyr fathere shot and a fellowe at Gravelines saw hysse onlie sonne fall before hysse eyes. Theyr grieffe shall onlie end at theyr own deaths. Mine shall stay wyth me until I am in your arms and thinke of thysse all as but a dream.

I gaze in the teeth of the gale as Recalde turns about. It moves me not – at first, how can I call myselffe friend to Wolf if I am easilie distract'd? Nowe the *Portugale* beats East twixt the greater island and the isle not two leagues to the north. There is but a wall of water and spray ahead of her. Thysse is a madnesse or courage to be be prais'd in song. The menne stand aft and watch our Admirale chase hysse doom. Hysse *San Juan* now rides the waves at speed. Surelie her keele touches the sand below. There are but thirty paces twixt her and the isle. Alle must be lost.

We stand amaz'd. and cheer. Recalde has loos'd anchore and rides safe. We loose our own and praie. The G-d of the waves is wyth Recalde. Hath he abandon'd the *Bautista*?

may vij, 1589

Mie poore friend Tomas is tooke sicke. I feare he has eaten the potatoe seed and hath an appallinge colicke. Michaele has ask'd that I look to him but mie skilles are not of the surgeone or medicke. Hysse children are wyth him. He is surround'd bie concern and love. It shall not avail him for I have knwen of thysse in the minifundias. A childe was tooke ill in the same way and all was tried – limone, herbes, prayer – even cidre. But the childe did not live.

may viij, 1589

I am tooke! Not wyth cholicke but as a prisoner! Michaele hath command'd that I be kep't in a small house – theye call them hyves. It is darker than night and too cramp'd to do anythinge but write bie daie – what little light there be. At least I have mie quille but I must shitte in thysse place and they give me onlie agua – no food. I do not understand what hath befall'n me but these people have offer'd nought but kindnesse. I am not afear'd.

may x

O mie love. I read those last lines writ two daies hence and see what innocence lies within. I was dragg'd from mie hut to attend Tomas's corpse. He was twist'd in a death agonie. Michaele was most calme. He said fewe words and look'd on me kindlie. If onlie I knew what must followe! I was taken to the well and amids't much clamouringe a declaration made – in Gael.

Mie few belongings were handed to me and the menne led me to the slip. I still did not guess mie fayte. The menne had two naomagh bound at the slippe's end and four of them bundl'd me into the first. Still I did not understand. Did they mean to take me to the maineland? Did they mean to cast me to the waves accus'd a murderere? The other menne climb'e into the second naomagh and we rowed as best could be attempt'd – first t'ward the maineland then at the flat island, Beiginis as they do call yt, the place of sheep onlie. Did they mean to execute me there? I did not thinke it soe for, rough and strong menne though they be, these islanders are peaceful, living onlie it would seem to work and protecte theyr families. The race was strong but these menne can seem stronger. We turn'd and I understood.

Tearagh't! I was being taken bak to Tearagh't! How I plead'd, all shame gone. I begg'd for mie lyffe - for some mercie. They answer'd notte and row'd on. I watch'd as the rock drew nearer and mie fayte determin'd. The waves abat'd nought though the menne knowest how to draw to the rock and leap for purchase. Thysse was not theyr intent. Two of the menne tied mie left arm to the side of the naomagh. Anothere jumped to the rockface and tied the rope to a jutting stone while theyr companion did hysse best to hold us steady as the second naomagh approach'd.

Then they were gone, alle four clamb'ring into the other boat as quicke as they dare. One last mercie? I was throwen mie sac and as the sea toss'd me agains't the rock mie companions, mie accusers, mie tormentors drew away.

Below the naomagh rides the surf still. Pound'd bie waves I see her beneath me from mie cave. Mie knife lies before me on the rough floor – mie captors at the last left me yt in the sac so cuttinge mie bonds should be easie. I thinke that they do not imagine me turning yt agains't mie owne flesh but such a daie may yet come. Forgive me.

I thinke on our journie – seldom have menne seen such sufferinge, such fear, such miserie. As we surviv'd, all else was throwen into newe perspective. The heroes of our lyfe at home, the sacrifices of the farmer that toyles or the menne that endure hardshippe in the picos gatheringe crops until the early hours, seem but small nowe. Friendshippe and valore nowe hath a diff'rent hue. Alonzo, Padraig, Wolf and myselffe play'd our part in an adventure that seem'd soe much greater than ourselffes.

I should be grateful to Felipe. He allow'd us to know the sea, courage beyond measure, companionshippe in the face of constant death. Perhappes thysse is the blessinge of the felicissima armada? Is there ought beyond? The simple community to be found in family lyffe, the joy of seeing our children play? I feare that findinge a common purpose in daies of peace and quiet would no longer be possible for any that survive thysse extravagant warre – even mie own unworthy sowle. Can I say thysse – I feare I would be bored even though I have lyfe still to be liv'd.

Was there ere such a place as thysse? A gaol wyth no sides, but fearful and complete trap nonetheless. I am surround'd bie beauty, movement, the noyse of the sea, the screeching of gulls – and mie owne terror and isolashunne. There are rembrances of Finestra – yet at Finestra the waves crash on three sides onlie. Yt is but a brieffe walk to othere menne - into fierce windes it is true – but wyth an aim that might be achiev'd, to meet wyth others again, to talk and drinke, to be warm at the fire of a taverna. There is no such hope here. The Blaskete lies to the East wyth no evidence of the menne I know to live there, the children at play, the womenne at work – washing, singing theyr lullabyes, tending the crops. Nought lies to the west but the Americas unless Bysse trulye exists and even that lonely isle must be a thousand leagues from here.

To the north lie the frozen lands, the wreckings of our great Armada, the bodies of mie dear friends. To the south, Spain. If I call out mie voice might, in the smallest part, be carri'ed to Finestra. You would hear words of love, of sorrowe and longing – and farewell.

Part Two

Being the woman's tale

Summer without you

This is tough. I'm writing but would rather talk. You must be talking – but not to me – and I hope you are writing. What would it be like if women talked to their men at war – every day or hour? Wars wouldn't last five minutes. I'd be calling you back before you'd left port.

G-d knows how my letters will reach you or yours me. Even letters to Felipe must take weeks. By the time he gets news the news has changed. As I write I know what love means. Because love doesn't change. Doing the thing – anything – your love wants is easy. Even writing gets easier. For women it's easier still.

Men are so ordinary. Do you have any idea how many men just want to come in a woman's mouth? Even my mother must do that for my dad – or he'd go off and find it elsewhere. And what does she get in return? He drones on about investments and the need to walk straight and tall. She listens out of love. It's not that he's boring – but fancy listening to him *every day*.

Was it such a difficult thing I asked though? For you not to leave me? I know how hurt you were. I did the freeing thing, gritted my teeth, and said,

"Follow your star." You looked shocked and all my hopes (that'll teach me) turned to ashes...Suddenly I had futures when every moment with you had been living in the now. And such futures – mere summaries of my past lives; being with people I didn't care for much, worrying about money, thinking (yes, thinking) that my breasts weren't big enough, my hair wasn't right, my conversation not sparkly enough (or too sharp when in the company of men) and all that nonsense I'd left behind by being with you.

Suddenly age was drowning me and today's sunshine would become tomorrow's rain – rain that couldn't lead to seeds springing to life, only mud.

Only mud.

And what did I do? I said: "Follow your star." Because I didn't think you would – you bugger. Did I complain? I know I'm complaining now but I'm so lonely and I have to plan a future without you. You can't hear me and if G-d wills that you come back I'll burn this diary – for love. I shall tell you I wrote something every day (so far, that's true) but the letters must have got lost. I don't write letters. What would they say? "The weather is fine. The baby inside me seems OK? I miss you.

I miss you. I miss you." If you love me as much as you say you do, your heart must burn too. ALL the time.

What should a woman ask of the man she loves? That he be faithful? Some chance. That he stays home by her side? She should ask nothing. If you shag someone else I'll be glad you're getting some. Pleased you're not lonely in bed. Well, if it's *in* a bed. In an ideal world a woman needs ask for nothing. The man would live to please her as she lives to serve him. Your precious Plato would approve. And he is precious. Horribly male but he did his best. I'm not sure I like it when he says that all this self control is meant to make men better governors. But men go to war again and again, so I'd rather have blokes with a bit of self respect. And war is inevitable. Even Felipe, for all his austerity, can't resist war.

You say you can't resist *me*. But that's when we're together. What must you be like when I'm not around? I wasn't enough was I? Even after you knew about the baby you yearned for more – more adventure, more of the world. My world is you and our baby to be. I sound weak and stupid. I'm not. I just hurt like hell.

Father has gone to *El Hallazgo*. It claims to be

the oldest taverna in Lugo. It's not that difficult; apart from those clustered around the main square there are only three. Still, a carving at *El Hallazgo* says it was built in 1389 – almost two hundred years ago. What must it have been like then?

"The same", you say. I agree except that was a century before the Inquisitores were set on us. Faji's family has always lived here. Many families have lived here for generations, having children, loving, dying and now some are driven to hiding their faith. But then, all that time ago, Morisco and Jew lived together in peace, no need to become converso. No need to hide. And *no* Fortunate Armada to take our men from us.

It's a beautiful day – so still, so sunny (of course). And here I am at peace, but writing. It's odd – I write more the busier I am and yet, today with all jobs done, I'm doing my best to conjure up the energy to scrawl. On days when father's demands are endless, house jobs relentless, food preparation never ending, I burst with energy and, somehow, write. Today, as Shabbus approaches, I'm finding it hard not to just sit and enjoy G-d's freedom to just be. Perhaps more words will come when we are kneading the chollah and I'm so rushed off my feet I can't sit down at all.

Perhaps I should try the newest drink – Alessandra told me about it. Coffee. It is quite extraordinary (says she). Very bitter, very dark, though Alessandra says I must try it with some molasses to make it more bearable (bearable! Can you believe it? A drink that must be made bearable.). It wakes you up immediately. She had a small cup yesterday and her body was alight! If it catches on, father must be careful not to have any before he goes to schule – he says he prefers to sleep while the rabbi chants away.

Mum wants to be there when the baby comes. So does dad but I don't think they'll let him. If you were here you could just come and sit with me. That would be enough. But, for now, it's all waiting.

Do you remember Jesus? Jesus Ramirez? He died last week. It was so sad. He and his brothers had grown old together looking after each other when their sister died. Their grove was so beautiful, all those limone trees and the special plants to attract the alauda. I don't know why they didn't marry anyone. Just happy I guess. But the younger brother, Javier was killed last year and Jesus and Martinez looked so miserable at the funeral. Martinez kind of shrunk in on himself and died of the cancre two monhs ago. Jesus had said that his only way out of misery was to do two things a day – one for G-d and one that might be dangerous. So last week, there he was planting new bushes for the alauda and then – get this – he climbed on to his roof to clear the moss. They found him curled up on the ground with his dog sniffing at his old body. He was smiling.

13th July

Writing, always writing. A diary? Of what? Actions, thoughts, contemplation (reciting prayers mostly) – how about the silences? Silence is an anathema – almost forbidden (unless you are a woman). We spend virtually no time alone, no silence. No time with ourselves, our dreams (except when dreaming). For a man to be silent is to be odd, quiet, reserved and – heaven forbid – "shy".

So we are surrounded by noise – chatter, "What did you buy? Isn't it lovely", old men telling children to be quiet in the LOUDEST possible voices, street vendors shouting, waitresses asking if you want more sac, all drowning out G-d's silence: the trees, birds, wind– even at home there is the same: mother saying, "Do this Beatriz, fetch me that Beatriz," father calling for his boots, dogs, "MORE sac."

And now? On the way to Nadela with the chit-chattering of children – and a scream that turns my hand-writing to scrawl. I bet you don't have the problem of four children singing *Fah, la la Lugo* at the tops of their voices. Still, their spontaneously-generated *Grandfather is a beast* brings a smile.

So now I'm in a store – *the* store – Tomas ben Adrim of Nadela. Talking to Tomas, a coast-lover trying – not very hard – to buy a place in Vigo. I tell him about the praza. I'm about to tell him about the fabulous meal Pasquale cooked for us there when I notice Tomas is still talking – to me. This is, of course, the female condition. We inhabit our mad worlds while people talk – we blink, smile, look concerned – a kind of facial dance, the steps long ingrained, but actually we aren't attending at all. At least not to what the other person is saying. We attend to our thoughts, reactions, conversational gambits. It's a social thing for us women, merely a matter of staying in the dance. How, we ask ourselves, do we keep this engagement going, pause, stop it, whatever? Then father taps me back to reality. The troop in the wagon want sweetmeats. Is this the interesting life of a woman – your woman? Lost in a fog of reflection in a village store while receiving demands for sweetmeats? Twenty minutes later I'm telling the nice woman in the taverna how interesting and diaryable my life is meant to be – and then the 'sweetmeats' punch-line. She smiles. We are clearly both mad.

Some hours later we are trundling down the road. Geese, gulls, alauda, the occasional carro with "Armada goods" emblazoned on its sides. What *are* Armada goods? I think I once knew but now the word means 'men', 'guns', 'grain'. Whatever – there are four syllables and the words sound strong – sure to impress.

We're listening to the children snoring. We had a long talk about silence (spot the irony?) – how quiet it can be at Cabo Fisterra if you ignore the gales. How some parts in the middle of Spain have no roads at all. Even around Madrid. Sevilla is so much bigger – and father says more civilized. He knows a couple who are serious travellers and, how about this, bird-watchers. They meet with others to seek out birds everywhere. The kind of people who think nothing of leaving a hot, idyllic beach on the Isla de Monteagudo (where they live – imagine!) to travel to some impossible rock in the sierra to watch vultures. Talked a bit about you a little. Mother invariably asks the same question, "Is he happy?" What can that mean? I say, "Yes" and haven't really a clue. "Seems OK and loving being part of the Fortunate Armada" – how likely is that? But, what if I say, "G-d forbid that over 500 miles away Isidore is probably unhappy." It will, in any case, pass. Unhappiness does.

Now we're passing a travelling theatre! No words on the side of the caravan but some glorious paintings of mysterious beasts. Down a hill – father asleep at the reins and I've no idea who's driving. Not me. I'm doing my diary. Cattle, to the left. A flock of sheep. You want a sheep story? In Alessandra's study group she met yesterday a man who had just sold his sanctuary at Marin. After 30 years he had said, "Buenos noces" And how much had he paid for it? In 1558, it had been a wreck of a farm house. The farmer wanted a lamb-bearing ewe. Deal. Hombre provides ewe, gets house and 30 years from a beautiful bolt-hole. Find myself drifting off into memories of our talks about bolt-holes – in Vigo, Ribeira, Tui.

By the way, this isn't just what diarists do – live in multiple times – we *all* do it. It's a feature of being alive and aware. The present doesn't exist, the future is unknown, the past ever-changing as we think it or write it down or stare at old sketches we did as school children. We dwell in our heads and it's a wonder so many carros and tumbrills can go so fast in such a narrow space without us all crashing off the road.

14th July

Wasted is the word. Memories of last night hazy – though I do remember walking into the taverna and telling a gorgeous innkeeper that I had been bet serious money that I couldn't find two nice young men and take them back to our hostel within five minutes. He called out in a HUGE voice explaining the challenge and, as the minutes ticked by, I started talking to Margaritas from Vilalba. "Bet" lost but without cover blown I went back to the hostel only to find that I had been followed by Margaritas! Tracked – by a woman. We left her trying to seduce two young men and went in to eat. Some hours later (after the "He'd fuck you as soon as look at you" comment from Alessandra – about me, talking about ben Adrim!) the wine took wild effect and I stumbled to bed. No sign of a lurking Margaritas so I slept til 7. Such indulgence.

Now some perspective. In a rather lovely church, only built in 1492, I know, I know, the year Isabella and Ferdinand declared the Inquisition and the expulsion of Jews from Spain. So here I am in one of *their* churches. Surrounded by the dead, dead stones, dead wood. And inscriptions to the departed – 1499, 1505, 1520, some small stones outside the door for children; aged 1, 4, 7, all dead, many long forgotten, their mourners also passed in to dust, earth, bringing new life. Life that also surrounds us. Trees, birds, flowers, chattering folk at Antonio's celebration.

Didn't I say? We've come to a celebration of the life of one of father's friends, Antonio, apparently *the* cook and best tavern keeper in Lugo for years.

Antonio died on 1st July.

Nicolas (Antonio's brother from Vigo) is speaking. Between his words there's a child, full of life, yelling, squawking, and giggling. Nicolas had only seen Antonio twice in the last 11 years having spent a childhood together in and around Lugo. A good – free – childhood followed by the walk to adulthood and the traps that a working life brings. Not for Antonio, I think. But still for Nicolas – apparently stuck on a treadmill of building bolt holes for island owning adventuroes.

There's a lovely story from Antonio's ex domus-maitre (it was THAT kind of school – well, it was Lugo) who first met Antonio in 1547. The story of young Antonio skipping school to go on a cattle husbandry field trip, despite not doing husbandry. His punishment? He had to cook for 13 fellow pupils and the housemaster, all under temporary shelter in the woods. The first time he cooked in public? Maybe...

Then more wine, more memories, more speeches – all in the sunshine back at the hostel.

15th July

Mother tells me it's late. Time to get up. Did my jobs then spent an odd morning in the square having G-d knows how much wine plus agua with mother's friend Martina. We talked of love, death, her confusion and more. I always respond in the same way to people who talk of being bewildered. A koan stolen from you:

Blessed are the confused
For they will find the way.
Cursed are the certain
That's the way they'll stay.

Now it's evening and I'm thinking about my monthly meeting with some of my girlfriends. I know, I know, "What do you women talk about?" The last time we met was on the coast and there in the heat we sat talking about the problems with their various men as if we were in Lugo. Then we got pissed – much more human.

It occurs to me that this diary is not remotely typical of women here – not least because I am, as promised, writing it. The crucial thing is why I'm doing it. Unlike the broken and the bereft in the majority, I write to keep a promise. At an age that means I am reasonably old enough to appreciate my time here but also a promise that catches me out regularly. Like today – walking home I suddenly realized my arm wasn't working properly, no doubt because of my manly bonfire making and wood sawing this morning. And, not inconceivably, related to the previous 36 hours of crowds, talk, travel, and drinking. And what did I worry about? Could I still write?

Let's see if I make it through this evening. I'm already dreading the journey back to the coast tomorrow night because that's going do for me on Wednesday when I should be holding my own up against goodness knows how many relatives who will want to know about the baby, marriage, are you a nice Jewish boy? All that.

Almost midnight and I'm only doing this because I'm so tired I can't stop. I'll stop.

16th July

Well, it's Tuesday. After a morning spent with Christina, Julio's widow, I picked the nephew up from Alessandra and – for no good reason – sat down to my diary. From being a proper aunt to scribbling in minutes.

Mind you, the morning had loads of agenda items: Julio, me being pregnant, how we are, *where* you might be, Julio's son who is about to lose his work at the farm and art, art, art. Christina is an art teacher who knows her stuff – loves

Leonardo and Raphael – but has never been to the Rome, Firenzi or Venizia. All planned; now she is retired. And Julio? Wouldn't leave the country for anything other than a trip to France with Bazia, his younger son. Happy, free and resistant to global exploration. An artist. A good man. A mensch, perhaps?

Thursday, 18th July

Doesn't time just fly? Somewhere between Tuesday and this morning (Alessandra's birthday), I travelled to Vilalba (father cancelled the journey to the coast – too hot), stayed at yet another hostel, ate dinner with Simone and, watched a ghastly theatre group stabbing at in-jokes about being a theatre group, woke up feeling dreadful and then talked to (with, at) Alessandra about my hangover. Then back to Lugo and, ultimately, home.

I almost got through a page of this before stumbling to bed. What was it – the travel, the new sac ("poor pregnant you" present from Simone), my age, the theatre? All of it, no doubt.

Alessandra opened her presents and I watched

in a daze. Lovely dress from father – I bet mother chose it.

As if that's not enough, I've spoken with Marco, just out of hospital with an enlarged heart (at least it's not broken), watered some very sad plants, picked limones, let the dogs out, had a glass of wine, wandered in to write this, left a message for Christina about Raphael, remembered to contact David about completing Julio's portrait (he was doing one of father, yes father, just before he died) and let the dogs out *again*. It's barely midday.

It's still barely mid afternoon and I'm listening to father:

"Has this Cervantes done his job well? Did you know Felipe threw him into prison after his disaster with the Fortunate Armada's provisions. He sounds like a very uncivil servant to me. They call him "el manco" because of an injury at Lepanto. Did you know that? It's only information in any case. And as my friend Dovid said, 'Information is not knowledge, Knowledge is not wisdom, Wisdom is not truth, Truth is not beauty, Beauty is not love, and Love is not music. Music is THE BEST.' Who can argue with that? How can we resist such alchemy?"

I'm not arguing. He's in major philosophical

mood. It's now late afternoon, still Alessandra's birthday – diarists of the world eat your hearts out.

My turn to be philosophical. It's a shame the Felipes of this world don't spend more time leering at girlswhodo instead of consorting with boyswhokill. Women though are increasingly defined by sex – the implication of all these just-the-same-face-painted-women is that they FUCK HARDER. And, er, that's it. Most men I know are as happy with sac and more sac. If all else failed they'd probably fuck the dog. Time to serve the paella.

Friday

It would be nice to say I can remember Friday (it's really now the Tuesday following) but apart from having an overwhelming sense that the morning took YEARS to get through, I don't. I managed to get to the market; Alessandra and I met up with Christina, listened to her talk about loss and then bought a bottle of aged sac for father. Christina seemed OK, if terribly thin. She was talking to Alessandra about someone she knows in Vilalba:

"When he met her she was 27, and he was 39. He used to positively bubble over with enthusiasm and could only talk of Dante Alighieri. That was exactly what interested her, along with love, which I'm sure her husband had abandoned. She was intellectual and, y'know, sensuous. She liked books, silk, diamonds and was secretly studying The Torah. She was like your sister (that's me!); curious about everything and insatiable in activity. (I bet she doesn't know just how insatiable I can be). The local women were dreadful. They called her plain. Senora Vimianzo said she was, 'Tall, sapless, narrow-hipped and narrow breasted, heavy arms, heavy legs, enormous feet...' And as for the charming Senora de Padron – I once heard her saying – really loudly so all could hear, 'The woman's a colossus in all her proportions. She has skin like a nutmeg grater.' But can women be trusted when faced with a woman who is intelligent, amorous, admired, and has conquered the most gorgeous man in town? I never met her, but I'd be surprised if she was anything but lovely."

You're the most gorgeous man in my town, honey. What can they all be saying about me? Still, they can't accuse me have having skin like a nutmeg grater. You love my skin – it must be OK.

"I hate Haifa," says Christina suddenly and manages to shake me from my day dreaming.

"Me too."

"And her mum is so fat."

"Her husband's a dog."

"Not as bad as Juan."

"No, I know."

"What's he up to?"

"Haven't you heard? He's with Louisa half the week, then back to Isabella."

"She's pregnant."

"Louisa?"

"No, Isabella. Mind you, it might not be Juan's."

"He's dreadful. You can hear him shouting at her through the walls. And they're not that thin. He uses terrible language. He must have something, though. Why does she put up with it?"

"Money and tobacco."

"Is that it?"

"How many men do you know with plenty of money and a tobacco plantation big enough to keep Lugo choking on the weed for a year? What else could she want? Anyway, she can't leave him. He's threatened to kill her if she does."

"He would too."

"Bernardo had a word with him. I think it was just manly stuff. You know, proving he wasn't scared even though he's older."

"How old is Juan, then?"

"About 25."

"Bernardo was brave."

"Bernardo's richer than Juan will ever be. Besides, he has men to back him up by the score."

Alessandra and I bid our farewells and I'd like to say I wandered off to meet my lover and we spent a delirious night fucking like rabbits – but I won't. But, only because I didn't.

So what did I do this morning? Ready for a tale of distraction? I woke up thinking, yes thinking, about writing. Write, write, write – right? Except I didn't. That's the trouble with thinking. It's easy to let the thinking leave you with the impression you've done something. So, while thinking about writing, I swept some leaves, saw the sun come up from the mist (beautiful, so beautiful), let father's dogs out, took father a little water (he complained – "You wake me up, for WATER!" Men!), helped mother make the spiced pears – quite a smell in the early morning as the vinegar always makes my eyes smart, decided to pack some things for our trip to the coast, decided to unpack them and take something different (the weather is deceptive, sometimes very cold in the mornings, sometimes warm by sun-rise), helped mother with the firewood, smelled the pears burning and rushed in to find father stumping around the kitchen yelling, "What's that terrible stink?", sat down for a minute looking at the dogs playing, realised they were worrying at a rat and had to sort that out (one very dead rat), then realised I must get on with what's inside my head and write it down. So I just did – Cervantes eat *your* heart out.

Winter without you

Whatever you're doing now I bet you're not thinking about a baby's bottom. I marvel at the change in me. I wanted you and I wanted your child. And presto! There I was full of fears about you leaving us, full of doubts about coping on my own – and more and more full of Jose. Then all the panic about the birth – could I do it? What if he changed his mind half way? I wouldn't have blamed him. This world is tough enough without being the only son of an unwed converso. He'd have been safe from men and their wars. No demands. No risk of being sent to die across the seas. Some of the Lugo boys have been sent to Vigo – and they're eight years old! It's disgusting. Have you seen any? Can you look after them? Are they dying like men? Or frightened kids? What else can they be?

And now I look at various ladies putting off the inevitable. For the sake of what? Dancing? Riding behind lords? So their figures will still look good in fancy clothes? Even when they have their little lordlings they'll have wet nurses to make sure their bodies still look trim – as if a bit of hard work wouldn't do the same. And they'll never know the fascination of babies' bottoms. Is it clean? Is it sore? Does it need a salve? And, oh, how beautiful it is. Perfect. Can men begin to imagine this feeling? You say you love my arse. It's the closest you'll get to knowing how mums feel about their children's bottoms.

I've just re-read that last bit and feel bad. Already I'm putting myself in the shoes of these poor women. What if they can't have babies? What if they daren't 'cos their men are away (like you)? You'd say I'm too kind.

Dunno where this came from but thinking about

figures and babies has moved me to – wait for it – a poem.

When the dust settles
I shall hold dear
The need to closer observe belly buttons
And that children are a gift from G-d.

Not exactly Dante I know.

Father called me in today. Just him and me. He had a map in front of him.

"Let's see where your brave lover-boy might be."

Then he softened.

"It's so difficult to know. They must be there by now but with winter storms and the like he could be anywhere."

He drew his finger through a whole mass of curved lines and numbers covered in drawings of leviathans and squid. Have you eaten squid? They look huge. The coast of England had some pretty ships and gentle waves. Father has lovely nails. They remind me of yours.

"If he's got this far, he'll have already faced the worst of the English pirates. Don't look so scared. We haven't sent the greatest fleet since the siege of Troy just to be stopped by a few English galleons.

They may have met up with Parma by now. Might even be in London choosing his reward. Do you fancy a town house or a little castillo? Don't cry, my love."

So, there I was, sobbing on my father's chest because his words had made me so happy. A castillo? That would do. *Anything* would do.

"He'll be on his way back soon."

Another hug, then: "Go and see to that grandson of mine. Your mother says his bottom needs changing."

February 13 and 14

I wrote the following for Jose. He can read it when he's older.

These are special days. On February 13 1588, Vigo's harbour showed every sign of being closed by snow. Snow! Your father will remember. Snow on the hills preventing carriages going through the passes. And those that tried to come down – such chaos, the poor horses sliding everywhere, tumbrills spinning round and drivers in a panic. There was even ice on the sea. This posed a problem.

Daddy (I love calling your father 'daddy') had arranged to meet me that day after noon. I had been staying with my uncle and hadn't seen Isidore for over a month. Meanwhile, your grandmother, who I had been living with in Lugo, was bound for Lisboa – weather permitting. I was at work in the kitchen wondering with my aunt what the worst possible outcome could be. Would Daddy be snowed out? Would he arrive, only to find that we couldn't meet because your grandmother's carriage was stuck in the snow and she was going to hang around?

I met him at the tavern in the praza. There he sat, drinking sac, looking thin – but lovely. He later told me that he knew at that moment he could only ever want me – even with my all-new hennae'd hair. A sac or two later and I took him home to my uncle's, then out for a fish dinner. Then home again – where you were conceived several times over. Valentine's Day was bliss. Vigo covered in snow, bagels and butter for an oh-so-late breakfast. He stayed a week. And here you are. These days are so special. I miss him so much.

Spring without you

Do men work this hard? It's bright, early. The alauda sings high above, the sun is well and truly up and I'm nursing a sick baby. Don't worry, he's OK, just a cold. But when he gets this snuffly, he can't breathe. Then he wakes *me* by getting all snotty and I start to panic that he *really* can't breathe.

Are all mums like this? Don't get me wrong. It's not that I don't smile. I smile when Jose smiles, when the sun shines – it's already warm and it's before six. I even smile when father tells me you're not worth the wait – he often does. In some ways, I'm not waiting. You're with me all the time – waking up, cooking, worrying about Jose, walking, sleeping. Sleeping is best. When I'm sleeping I don't quite know what's going to happen. When I think of you or your bloody adventure while I'm awake I try and control my imagination. And you know exactly where *that* usually leads – some version of you licking my bottom while I come. But when I'm asleep I can't control what's coming – even if it's me! I might dream of the house – father, mother, anything. And then from somewhere, deep inside me, you appear. These visions can be awful. You can be starved, thin, smashed up, broken – once even dead. But they can be incredible too. We make love everywhere. Behind the wood shed, in the kitchen, twice (twice - note to self; I must want this) on tables with you dressed like a rich man. The second time you looked dressed for temple. I tried to be demure and after a whole twenty seconds I still had my kit on. Then you were all over me. It turns me on writing this.

Where are you, you fuck? No doubt you are sitting somewhere having a wank. Typical bloke. You can be thousands of miles away, facing G-d knows what and you'll need to do it won't you. Sorry – busy, tired, resentful...

How can people have so many children if they don't have servants and decent child-care? This is knackering. He's a lovely boy but his mum is exhausted with the simplest things – changing, feeding, more changing, playing. All those things men think are straightforward. And he wants me all the time. ALL the time. When he's not yelling for food, he's wanting to be picked up.

I don't mind really – he's so gorgeous but a live-in help would be nice.

It's just not that easy here with a child – on your own at least. I get stared at – a lot. Blokes smirk, even the ones with women at their sides. Women look at me suspiciously – like I'm after their men. Chance would be a fine thing with Jose in tow. My lord has warned me I'll be easy prey and, no doubt, soon the subject of 'sympathetic' women's gossip. You know: "Poor dear. Her man is fighting for Felipe and adventure, and here she is all alone with a baby to raise as best she can. Shame. And shame on her."

Shame on them too. Mind you, the men can be worse. They don't just stare. I saw a grey, short-haired woman today. And, as she passed, two (two, no less) men leered: "Nice arse," so she could hear. Is that supposed to be seductive? She smiled and did her best to look disdainful but they were *all* thinking the same thing. Her too.

At least I'm not bored. Men and women doing what they have always done. A child to nurse, clean, smile for (and at – boy, he can make me laugh). Not like you with your attempts at sagacity and so called philosophising – like when you suggested practising celibacy based on some Platonic ideal or other. That lasted all of a half day

– I think I fell pregnant during one of your more intense bouts of celibate living! You once said that Plato suggested doing bad things so you could master the urge to repeat them. Your tongue was in my bottom at the time. I didn't notice a lot of self-mastery on your part.

I have a new game. I pretend your tongue is inside me and try to sit still. My father has caught me squirming away with my belly muscles getting tighter and tighter. I'm sure he thinks I've got worms. Mother even had a word:

"Beatriz, are you OK? Your father says he keeps catching you trying to sit still but agitated like a fish on the line. And smiling! I ask myself what a young woman who twitches so much can have to smile about. And I think you must be praying for Isidore's return and imagining his body as he twists to dodge arrows and shot. You smile as you imagine him safe, no?"

I do wonder if she knows what sex is. Alessandra knows.

"You're thinking of him inside you again," she said in the middle of a major piece of squirming. What it is to have a nosey sister. If only she knew what part of you I imagine inside me – and where.

It might be wonderful to be bored just for a

moment. I was never bored with you – making love, you working or talking about your philosophers and Felipe's great plan. There's no boredom here – just a kind of mindlessness. I work, wash, play with Jose, change Jose, worry that Jose's not breathing when he's asleep, talk to mother if I don't think he's eating enough (he is). He's growing fast and I talk to Alessandra about if he's the right size. I'm sure he's OK – he's going to be tall. I do all of this in an unfocussed kind of way but it's never dull. It might be quite something to face boredom every day. What must it be like to be a lady? Not sure which dress to wear or which powder would suit.

"Is it this season that we move to blue, or next?" "Perhaps, a little more rouge to highlight my hair, don't we agree?" "Shall I try the Parfum Orientale today?" "Silk or crinoise with the heat?" "A parasol, perhaps?" "So little time, so many decisions." "I really must get one of my maids to lay out the summer dresses. They're far too outmoded for this year's salon."

I'd go mad. My lord Bernardo would have me weighed down with choices like these. Boredom? Incarnate. But, maybe I wouldn't be so weary.

Father asked us to wait for him at the ninth gateway today. The ninth! You know what that means. My lord duly appeared, riding at hound. For bears, I wouldn't be surprised. He's a fine sight – a bit full of himself, but he would still make a fine husband. Nice arse too. Are you jealous yet? Father went over to him and Bernardo recognized him immediately. These men have met before! Father pointed in my direction and Bernardo smiled and raised his cape – a flash red number (like blood).

Two donas walked by – you know how they do it, managing to look pious and disapproving even though you can hardly see their faces. Bernardo kept his cape raised until they'd gone – more efficient than having to raise it twice I suppose. He gave a little flourish. Meant to be ironic but it was lost on the donas. I'm sure some people find him really attractive. I do my best to fancy him but it's hopeless. You can't *decide* to want someone. You either do or don't. Bernardo has no shame, not that much humour and is probably only attractive to fifteen-year-old, starry eyed, girls.

But he does have money – and land. I could have enough dresses to last two lifetimes. I'm sure father intends me to marry him. He knows conversos aren't safe, even in Lugo – and there's still tolerance here. Our son would still be Judio. So would any children I had with Bernardo, but only in the strict sense. They would be raised in the church of Bernardo, Felipe and the rest. It doesn't matter. What's the main message anyway – that we should thank G-d for life and treat strangers as we would be treated. Life is still life for all of us. I'm grateful for every day of it. And I miss you so much.

I just had one of the first – if not *the* first – serious talks with mother. Out of the blue – and it is blue today – azure wherever you look. Much too bright to look straight up. We were sitting in the shade, Jose fast asleep, and mother says:

"Do you ever think how mad our laws are? All made by men, for men. Men can carry arms, kill on command, leave us behind while they fight for Felipe. While they're free to do all this killing, we can't make new life, unless it is with a husband - she looked hard at me at this point. Can't walk out bare headed, eat well or work in any way on Shabbus.

We can't even touch our blessed husbands when

we're unclean. Ants have more freedom!"

We watched an ant scurrying this way and that. He was looking for food, oblivious to religion, Felipe, the Fortunate Armada – even mother and me. She's never said anything like this before. She usually goes on about how difficult it must be for me to manage Jose on my own (it is) and how I should find a man with money and land to keep me safe. Safe from what? Men and their warring ways? It's too easy to blame it all on men. Fernando was kinder. But it was Isabella who pushed for the Inquisition. And she already had children. She knew how precious life is. Those first incredible moments when the child arrives and ALL you care about is that he is safe and whole.

I didn't believe I could love someone more than you – Jose changed all that. I would give my life for him, no problem. No hesitation. I'd even give up my life with you. Maybe that's what mother frets about – she thinks I don't understand how Jose must come first. But I do. I know it in my bones.

I'm getting worse. I'm often now just writing about what I do, even when all I'm doing is thinking about writing – then trying to find a moment to commit thought to paper. Just for you.

Am I trying to be you? You once said we are all each other anyway. The rich, the poor, men, women, children that play – or cry, or get in trouble (for playing, for crying). What did you mean? Are we really the same? I don't see anyone else writing. Maybe they find a quiet space to do it. But writing's just doing. I don't think we all *do* the same. Inside, maybe inside – is that what you meant? The woman sitting opposite, the children sitting intent on something in the dust (a beetle, I think). What are they feeling? What fears do they have? The dona making her way across the square – does she fear her G-d is watching. She looks proud – does she fear her pride is a sin? The woman sitting across from me looks a little fearful. Of what? Is she pretty enough, too fat, too thin, worried her lover no longer cares? Is that the sameness, then? Fear. Not fear of the same things but just fear? The children sit quietly. Do they fear retribution if they play? And when they play – is the fear gone? Does the woman across from me find contentment and freedom in play with her lover? (Outrageous! How can I know she has a lover at all? Well, we are all the same!) But is that it? We all live in a cycle of contentment and fear?

Words tumble in my head. I think it's easier to

just write them down as I think. Or at least I want to, but a call comes – for water, soup, even washing. You might be on a great adventure but try being a woman for a week. The words vanish as soon as father calls out and I forget what I wanted to say. Our baby is pretty exhausting too. All feed, no sleep for mum, then off he goes and I'm just about to drop off and dad yells for something else. It's going to be worse if I marry my lord and he wants sex. I really want to tell him there's only one man for me – and it's not him.

Don't get big-headed honey. Our first time is still pretty unbelievable though. You said you were nervous. How do you think I felt? And you didn't give me much chance to see you. I'm not sure I've seen anyone get under the covers so fast. Still, what followed wasn't bad. I think I told you to slow down but it was fine – really fine. Then you came again and I thought, "Aye, aye, what have we got here?" Bloody stud, that's what. And as for your tongue – well! We should market it – I'll make my fortune. Then I forget where my parchment is.

We went to the taverna today. Not quite proper I

know. Mother in her finest. "Man-catching" gear she calls it. Not for her. She's loved dad forever. She tolerates everything you hate in him – his obsession with property, money, security. The way he calculates a man's worth by how much land he owns. Or the way he insists we all eat properly, sit properly, must treat our bodies as temples. Your body seems good enough to me but father worries you don't walk as well as you might and thinks you drink too much. A bit rich from a man who takes *aguadiente* as he breaks fast before sun-up.

So mum's in her glad-rags, Jose has his bonnet. He brings such smiles. It's all part of mother's man-trap. She wants a man for me who'll smile at Jose *before* he looks at my body. That would be a trick in Lugo! We sat next to a seigneur and his lady in all their finery. And what did he do? Stared at my tits with one of those lingering "scan up you down and back again" stares. And he was vain. Do men get more vain with age? His hair was cropped to make it look like it wasn't receding (it was). And dyed, of course. But his paunch! That wasn't receding. It was enough for two.

She wasn't exactly trim but she had some self respect. Her hair was hennae'd and mostly covered up – but not powder'd like his. It's a wonder his skin didn't suffocate. What does she see in him? Whatever happens in bed?

If mother's plan is for me to forget you, sitting in tavernas isn't going to do it. She says me having an amore de lonh is becoming an embarrassment. She swings from saying men are a liability (except dad, of course) to hissing,

"If you won't have our good lord, then at least try to get a man who's not forever rhapsodizing about love and gallivanting on the high seas."

That's you. Are you gallivanting? G-d, I don't even know if you're alive and mother says you're on a jaunt. It's hard to tell what's happening. There's no talk of the Fortunate Armada nowadays. People go about their business as usual. At least the women do. There are so few bloody men. Felipe has seen to that.

You really don't think like a woman do you (sorry, critical again)? I wonder if any man does. What do you tell me about when we talk? How much you love me. How much you desire me. A fair bit about your hopes and dreams for us in the future. You tell me I turn you on. Do you realise it's the talking that turns me on? I'm sure you could be pretty ugly and it wouldn't matter. You listen to me, make me laugh, talk seriously to me about important things. Socrates got it right, I think. You appeal to my need to be respected. But why aren't you HERE?

The truth is I just wasn't enough for you was I? I know you need to be free to follow your star. But I thought we would do that together. Some of us women love stars too you know. Now I'm alone and missing you and the future looks empty. I need to do what I can for the boy. My dad will arrange some work for me. Who knows I might even marry our dear lord – it'll only give me some kind of safety for the future. At least he's HERE. I don't want to be with him. I want to be with you. If you are dead, at least I know I'll be with you one day. Life is empty without you.

Young men here all seem stupid – snatching kerchiefs from their girl-friends or puffing out their chests – I love your chest. I don't know what they have to show off about. They haven't left to take England for Felipe – G-d I sound like a man now. At least they're alive. We'll never be together will we? There'll never be an "us". This bunch of kids has more chance of ending up together than you and me. Even if you come back you'll be changed forever. A man of peace who's killed. A Jew who worships life but has seen so much death.

How long would we have? Three months before you were off again? Long enough for me to get breathless just thinking about being in bed with you. Long enough to get pregnant. Then what? Off you'll go and I'll have two children to cater for. And explain their dad is following some romantic dream of seeing the world – good and bad. It's different for me. Jose makes me happy. He's enough. I work hard to keep him clean, fed and safe. Lugo is a haven. If you know how to look it *is* the world. People meet, fight, break up, gossip, struggle in the fields, get jealous – it's all here under your nose. And it takes as much courage to stay as it does go – swanning off, mother calls it.

A man has just passed with his baby. I wish that's all he needed to satisfy him. I bet his wife is at home with five more. Maybe she's dead and he's using the same bait that mother prepares for me most days. A child to make women smile. It's working too. I'm smiling. He's leaning over Jose. Cheek.

"He has his mother's eyes"

"And his grandfather's."

"Can I join you for a drink?"

"Is that the time?" says mother. "I must get back to make your dad something to eat. Don't rush Beatriz and don't forget to keep Jose out of the sun."

As if I would. And she's gone. Just like that, leaving me to make small talk with the first catch of the day.

There is such life here. Such variety. You see it in the children playing, the limone trees, the dogs chasing their tails, and the women – those that aren't sullen. A made up girl (Girl! Listen to me, she must be at least 16) sits sullen though her eyes betray her. They are deep brown and flicking all the time to her man in a kind of love dance, the steps uncontrolled but precise. He sits quiet, very brown. Very weather-beaten – a tarre? Oh my G-d, he stands – with her help – on his only leg. Is he from the Fortunate Armada?

"Your pardon, sir."

"Yes."

"I'm sorry to ask but have you been to sea, perhaps for Felipe?"

The man suddenly looks scared – courtesy replaced by fear instantly.

"Who are you? Can't you see he's not well?" says his consorte.

“Don’t fret, Juanita” –what a beautiful name for such a beauty – “She means no harm.”

He turns to me:

“I sailed with Recalde. I have that honour – and this.” He points to the space where his leg should be.

“I’m sorry, I didn’t mean to pry – you see I’m concerned for....” (What do I call you – my lover, my child’s father, just a man?)

“So many are.” Now he looks kindly. “Does he have a name?”

“Isidore.”

There are a few moments silence. I hold my breath. The world, the market, all stands still in the midday haze.

“I knew one.”

I’m reeling, more than giddy.

“A small fellow, with such blue eyes. I last saw him in Lisboa.”

“Short? Blue eyes? My Isidore is tall. His eyes are brown.”

I feel darkness enclosing me. It’s not you. How could it have been? And even if it was – Lisboa! That’s before the Armada set sail.

"I'm sorry. I met many men called to sea by the adventuros or by Felipe, and only one Isidore."

"What happened to your leg?"

The girl, Juanita, gives me such a look.

"I heard it was easier to swim with one leg, less drag in the water. So I had it cut off."

"You're not serious."

He is smiling now, the frost from Juanita gone. He must be easy to love.

"No, it was cannon shot, at Gravelines. I don't remember much. One moment we're waiting for the tide. The next there are fire ships everywhere. Men panicking. A tremendous noise. Then silence and darkness. When I woke I was being tended by a Frenchman and his family – my leg screaming agony where they'd cauterised it. I didn't have any idea how long I'd been there, or how I'd got there. I passed out again. I was woken up and told that some of Parma's men were approaching the farm. The family gave me food to take and I joined about a hundred others on their way to Holland."

"But that's north."

"North, then south again, then through France. I haven't seen the sea for months."

"Come Dovid, we must go."

"Dovid? You're a converso?"

"Of course, how else do we survive?"

"My Isidore also."

They turn and walk a few paces. As I look, he stops, turns, seems to think and smiles. He returns, leaning on Juanita.

"I did hear of an Isidore, senora - a Jew"

This time my heart stops.

"A strange tale. Some men from the Bautista got into some kind of fight on the Wight Isle. It's very close to the English shore. The rumour spread that these men had landed and gone to a tavern."

"An English tavern?"

"Of course. The Wight Isle is English. Though I suspect that many strayed from the Fortunate Armada. It is a small, peaceful place. Some Portugaise already live there. The tavern keepers don't mind who is paying for their ale."

"And the tavern story?"

"It's not much. And you know how re-telling changes the plot. A curious group of friends from the *Bautista* – an Irishman, a Portugaise, another from Spain and this – maybe your – Isidore fell to fighting, lost and fled. This would have been before the battle."

"Battle?"

"I call it battle – it was more of a rout but it was

our *only* battle."
"We must go."
Juanita is pulling at my messenger's sleeve and I stand transfixed. I can't help but call:
"When, tell me when?"
He turns one last time.
"Last August."
August, August! Six months ago.

Autumn

OK, are you ready for this? All I've written is true. But you can lie by omission, can't you. I got tired touching myself. I needed YOU. Inside. Then I had a breakthrough. We're not married, you are G-d knows where and I'm up for it. It's not like I didn't have offers. Your brother was attentive for a day or so. Even *my* brother offered.

"If it's just a shag you want, sis, I could have a go."

I turned him down but it made me think. Is it just a shag I want? Is that seemly? So, as of three weeks ago, I have two lovers. It's interesting stuff too. Chavez I is taller than you and hates being tall! He says it makes him look odd in a crowd. I didn't point out it's odder he didn't join the Armada. Still, he has some money – probably bribed someone. He has a nice body too. Doesn't make me sigh like yours but it's not bad for an older man. Are you shocked? Wait for this. My other Chavez is younger than you and fat! Well as fat as you can get on a diet of nothing. But he's kind, attentive and, I think, grateful. It's been lovely having a grateful man in my bed. Chavez I is married. He hesitates when he speaks. Words like Lugo come out L-u-u-u-go (he almost spits the end). I told him I found it sexy – I do.

He comes across as a bit shy in public, nothing like the older men strutting with their paunches on show. He says he was impossibly shy 'til he was about fifteen. Then he decided to just open his mouth and see what happened. You can't really predict when it's going to be worse. It can be hilarious in bed. He'll start some love talk, then gets a bit stuck and before you know it he's screaming, "I-I-I-I'm c-c-c-c-com-m-mING!" And he does, with me in fits.

I haven't made either of the Chavez's public - I'm only telling you.

Father keeps telling me to talk to Jose and then wants help with his packing – he leaves for the shore tomorrow. I do talk to Jose but it's pretty negative stuff – "If only your dad was here to give a hand." That sort of thing. Your arms round me would help – but so would walking the baby at night to give me a little peace. Tell you what – you come home safe and we'll talk about having another – just as long as you can prove that you're not just another of these men who expects the woman to do all the work.

This is a bit embarrassing. Bloody Chavez I's wife found out about us. Ghastly scene too, apparently. Imagine. Then Chavez and I are sitting on the terraza having a glass of sac (he calls it post-sack sac) and Senora Chavez turns up with baby in tow (no, he hadn't told me about the baby).

"You want my husband, senora? Then you take Toni also!"

And there I am with a surprised little boy in my arms gazing at me with his father's eyes. Blue, very unusual here, but lovely like ice.

Then another set of blue eyes looking at me, plaintive as hell before turning to his wife:

"Paramore!"

Paramore! And Chavez I is off in pursuit leaving

me with baby Antonio in my lap and two glasses of sac.

How slowly time moves – when you're waiting. Mother says this gets both harder and easier as you get older. If you are lucky enough (lucky?) to be very ill (get this!) she says time stands still. An hour feels like a day, all your energy focussed on where it hurts, if it feels a little easier, if you can manage to eat, drink, stand, working out if it's day or night. If you are less lucky life is filled with waiting – to die.

"Sorry about that Maria." I look up and see a charming looking man. He has spoken – with the oddest inflection, almost distortion – to a *very* twisted and stunted girl. Isn't it terrible how we judge by appearances? There he is; tall, good looking, short-cropped grey hair and, just as I was building up to a little flirting (as you do), he realized that the younger woman couldn't sit easily at the table. So he stands, just about manages his brief apology, and helps her sit. And there he is, kindness personified, and barely able to string four words together.

As subtly as possible (Alessandra calls it 'staring with intent') I look closer. Half the back of his head just isn't there. Shot away? Something from birth? Whatever the cause, this lovely man has a great dent where his skull should be. Who cares? He is kind, good looking and has a gentility that's quite something to witness. His hands are shaking – he can't control them – and he peers around, taking it all in (but not me; he doesn't look at women as so many do – a blessing).

I read back what mother said and the man's nobility shames me. My life actually seems to get fuller and fuller (like my bed – naughty!). If I'm not fucking Chavez II, I'm changing the baby. If I'm not helping mother, I'm bloody writing – your fault. And though time stands still, it still presses on. I am amazed – AMAZED – at just how much I do in a day but it's like every second crawls to meet the future. Even now – a moment's peace – and I'm writing to try and explain how S – L - O – W it all is. I'm waiting here for Chavez I. After our little incident he crawled back, full of pleadings and, after all, he is a good shag. It passes the time.

What if I was sitting here and you came? Now? What direction would it be from? Would you be with others? Alone? Tired? Wrecked and ruined by the sea and your adventures? Utterly broken?

With a woman? I wouldn't put that past you. Do any of the people in the square know what I am going through? Of course. There are many like me. They wait. They get on with their lives. Their hearts slowly close.

"Hi."

"Oh my G-d!"

Chavez stands before me. Just for a second I thought... Fuck.

I just had a lovely talk with my sister (isn't it odd how I write to you as if you can hear me – or even as if you are still alive? Are you?). She asked if I ever talked to my friends about sex. Something was obviously on her mind! She said that most of her friends only ever mentioned it in passing – you know – "It was good/bad last night" – that sort of thing. She was tired of so many of her mates just talking about men as "hopeless" (not just in bed) or saying their lovers were never interested in serious talk, at least not with women. So, even though the men think the women are talking about them all the time, they rarely get a mention.

So sis finds herself talking about the state of the world or – you'll hate this – feelings. Sis said it would make such a nice change to have a good talk about something genuinely serious – like the state of your love life. After all this is going to be the man you wake up to for half your life.

Anyway, I found myself talking about Chavez I and II's dicks and how different they are. She said she had never talked about men's cocks before and wondered if any women did. I said it was probably about having two men pretty close on each other so the first one was more on your mind. I don't know if it's the sort of thing I usually notice. Shoulders, yes. Bottoms, of course – yours isn't bad. But dicks? She said she'd been so faithful for so long she kind of assumed men's equipment was much the same. Well, it's not. Chavez I is a big boy (do you really want to know this?) and it's kind of soft, even when he's inside. C II's is much leaner even though he's a fatter man - and really brown.

Alessandra was shocked and wanted to know more. Truth is, I drifted on to talking about bums and tongues at that point (you win again) but promised I'd give her a full report next time I see her.

I must be going mad. I spent four or five hours in bed with Chavez I and spent half the time inspecting his parts trying to make notes for my sis. It's quite something size-wise – I even tried weighing it in my hand for a while but he liked that so much it got harder than usual so we did the next thing.

Then, guess what (you're going to hate this)? Straight round to C II to make sure I remembered Chavez I well enough to compare. I was right about the leanness – it makes the veins really stand out. The brown-ness reminds me of some of the slaves we see on my lord's estate. I reported all that to Alessandra – who looked horrified then gave me a run down on her husband. It's bent at the end! She hadn't really noticed before but she says there's a definite kink in it. I asked her how it felt but she's so used to it that she couldn't remember anything different.

Then she said she'd brought it up with her friend Clara. Apparently she looked really shocked then went on about Anjelo who has *el mejor* body in Lugo – in every way. He's built like a stallion and has balls so big each one just about fits into the palm of her hand.

Course that gets me thinking about you – then I remember. You do have lovely balls. You used to love it if I put one of them in my mouth. At which point Alessandra says:

"You've drifted off, Beatriz. Were you thinking about Isidore?"

"It was you talking about balls."

"How are his?"

"I can't tell you about that. It's too intimate."

"But you didn't mind describing Chavez I and II."

"I know, but they don't count."

"Oh my G-d, this really is love isn't it?"

"Tell me about it. It's like walking round with a hole where my heart used to be."

"How come you're sleeping with the others then?"

"I don't know [if this was a play the stage direction would have said *beseeching wail* at this point]. I'm just going off my head with loneliness."

"So you don't really like the sex?"

I was about to spout: "No" and I realised what a lie that would have been. I do like the sex. It's not you, but they are fun in bed, their bodies are pretty good and WHAT AM I SUPPOSED TO DO while you're off saving the world?

"Come on B, be honest."

"The sex is the best part. Chavez II can be a bit

dull but in bed he'll do all sorts. It's great."

"Like?"

"He'll just lie on top of me sometimes. It's lovely having a man's weight on me. Really warm. Fantastic after a good fuck."

"What would Isidore say?"

"He knows I love that. We used to do it most times we slept together. Anyway, I tell him."

"How?"

"In my dreams, in my head while I'm walking along with mother. Sitting in the sun. And the diary."

"Diary?"

"I keep a diary for when he gets back so he'll know what's happened."

Sis looked really sad. She doesn't know if you're alive either. But she thinks you're dead. Don't be dead. Not 'til you've put your weight on me one last time.

Now I'm sitting in the square, eavesdropping on a converso dressed like a peacock and his friend, dowdy but sweet looking.

"He threw you out?"

"Out?"

"He threw me out."

"But it's not his house!"

"They're not married."

"Bet he doesn't pay any rent either."

"He doesn't even live there."

"What?"

"He lives in Vilalba."

"And he threw you out?"

"He was bigger than me."

"My G-d, everyone's bigger than you."

He sits, scalded. I bet he's wondering if it's true. He looks a bit taller than his mate but more gaunt. Fragile, even.

"You're just scared."

"Of?"

"Everything."

"I'm not."

"Ok, prove it. See that woman?"

The peacock points to a quiet looking women sitting with a child three tables away.

"Go up to her and say: 'This is my last night in Spain, I may not return. Will you sleep with me?"

That's rich. His last night in Spain! If he'd been an *adventuro* he'd have gone when the Armada sailed. And most of the ordinary men from the villages were taken months ago. What's his excuse for still being here? What's your fucking excuse for *going*?

Why do people, well women, look down as they walk? Shame (not an obvious converso in sight)? Do they fear stumbling on the cobbles (they say that so-called true believers fear the cracks between)? It's not mud (it's been dry for weeks). Fear of lustful glances (their own or men's)? Perhaps they're older than they look and have fallen before. You know, legs and lace akimbo for all the world to see. The men are different. They stride – s..t..r..i..d..e – purposeful, resolute.

Well, that's how they want to look. They say women can only do one thing at a time but I see these women thinking about the market, gossiping as they walk, worrying about their children *and* examining their feet. That's it! It's men who only think of one thing. Their striding says it all. No children to feed, no petty domestic frivolities to distract them from their groins. The groin is king.

Now I'm back in the sun with Alessandra.

"He still hasn't seen me with, like, no make up. Even in bed, I've got a little powder on. We had a fall out last night – we were play fighting and he gave me a love-bite and I yell: 'That's out of bounds.' Y'know, dignity and everything. Miguel and Ali are going to go on about it – the curiosity of kids knows no bounds. I've got to wear a scarf all day – and it's so fucking hot. Still, it's good if you don't see each other all the time. I mean, what would you have to talk about with your man around all the time? G-d, I'm sorry Beatriz."

I must have looked like I felt. Empty, sunk, miserable as sin.

"It's OK. I talk to Isidore all the time."

"You do? How?"

"It's gonna sound pathetic."

"No, go on."

"You know. In my dreams. When I see something interesting, I'll write it down for him then just talk out loud like he's here. Then the same night it will come to me while I'm asleep so I'll say it again."

My lovely sister looked long and hard at me. I thought she was going to say something *simpatico*.

"You're right, that's pathetic."

And we sat there laughing 'til the tears rolled down our faces.

Eventually, I said: "I even write him poetry."

"Can I see?"

"You're only gonna laugh."

"S'not a crime is it? Anyway, I like poetry. Let's see."

So I showed her, risking all – well, at least a little

literary criticism. I showed her *Lovely One*.

Here you go, guess who I wrote it for: Mr I'llbebacksoon?

Lovely one

If it has been a beautiful day,
the stars are breathtaking
and you are at peace with the world,
perhaps you won't feel annihilated.

You could try...
emancipated
intoxicated
animated
elevated
exhilarated
titillated (try de la Vega)
dominated (try me)
elongated
marinated (first taste please)
domesticated (hmmm)
exfoliated (you'd love that)
epilated (that'll hurt)
stimulated (me again)
levitated (don't try this without me)

inebriated
vindicated.

And just think. After the dust has settled, you won't have to feel...

subjugated (unless you ask nicely)
manipulated
delegated
obligated (only to love)
eliminated
contaminated
terminated
or cremated.
unless you want to.

And however you feel, at the end of the day, always feel loved.

Tell me this, Mr Smartass writer. Does writing come from unhappiness or joy? I'm so bloody unhappy so much of the time. Then I write (to you, about you) and it's gone – until the next time. So I write again. I don't get bored doing it – do you? Will you if you ever read this? Don't you dare. This *costs* me. So fucking much. Well, apart from the cost of the ink – hee, hee.

The scary thing is being so bloody efficient – a constant doingness. Most of the women round here seem to be the same. Mum sure is. I walk to the kitchen carrying a plate – then realise I could carry more. So I go back all of ten steps to balance a few more plates and a glass or two. In the kitchen I spot last night's glasses (father, not me) so I empty the dregs. As I wander back I need – sad, or what? – to write this down so I look for a stylo and ink. Why? For a famous tome like de la Vega? For posterity? Just to do. Do, do, bloody do. It's all doing.

When I am finally dead I shall rest and the madness will stop infecting the others around me like Alessandra. They can relax a little – well, except mother. They can stop feeling ashamed that they do less. Of course, they're doing more than enough for them. And for me. Because I don't do this stuff for admiration or to inspire. I just do it. And one day I shall rest.

Do you get much rest, my love? Is it all blissful idleness? Or are you constantly clambering up masts (be careful), sluicing (do you sluice?) down decks and all that? I hope you are sitting in a tavern talking quietly with friends. There may even be peace on the glorious Armada – I pray G-d there is. I don't think my grandmother stopped even when she was dying. The occasional burst of pulling weeds from around her precious flowers, including the times when she could barely get up from kneeling. We all thought her mad but she seemed content, almost free of pain.

When she couldn't go outside any more, she'd give mother instructions on where to weed, where to store the cuttings – as if mother didn't have enough to do with my brother and sis and me (and dad, of course). Did she want peace? I think peace meant death for her. We may be the same. I just want to rest - but I can't.

When death came for grandmother, her body fought back. With every rasping breath it fought. Mother held her and cried like a baby 'til she was at peace. I have her disease – not the cancre G-d willing – the disease of doing.

I'm on a beach. A beach! Father decided we would have a day by the sea so here we sit, no shade, staring at the Isles des Cias waiting until he has had his fill of half naked women and their children

– all playing on the sand. Where are you? Do you have your own beach yet? Are there women? When you look at other women, do you compare them with me?

I try the comparison stuff but it doesn't work. Chavez II is here. He's OK and there are a few others around us – mostly old or broken, all of them dark brown. Many are thin, nearly all are bald and some have muscles like yours. It's hard to make sense of, but I kind of look *through* them. I only see you, the comparisons are gone in an instant. No desire. Well, a little when Chavez flaunts himself – for my mother, I think! The dog. But having Chavez is easy. I could have any of these men – you taught me that. And a lifetime of mother saying: "Beatriz, be choosy – you can afford to wait."

My guess is that most of these women could have who they want, at least for a night. But I want you – our 'animal magic' as you call it. Bit weak for you I thought, but, hey, it *is* magic and we are animals. You inside, licking, astride, between, behind, touching my skin, my hair, eating me alive. Shocks run through me and we are one.

"Beatriz!" I look up and a very cross father is standing over me.

"What in G-d's name were you doing?"

"Writing and day-dreaming, father."

"Writhing, more like. There are people staring."

There are too. I drifted away and started touching myself on instinct. Now I'm so wet and don't know whether to laugh or hide. If you return – you must – we shall make love for days. Neither of us will walk for a week. G-d I just said: "Fuck me" out loud. Chavez is grinning like a fox.

This love business is exhausting, however you look at it. I miss you and it wears me out. I try Chavez (I or II) and I'm bloody well thinking of you. Well, not *every* second, but you know what I mean. And when I'm with you – it's a wonder I even remember. Content and exhausted all in one.

Mother's attitude has something to recommend it. She says she often can't remember what all the fuss was about and gets so much more from gentle chats with her mates. I have seen them all standing – in full sun – in the market square talking, listening, absolutely engrossed – about what? Alessandra has two friends who keep lists. Lists! Beatriz (not me, my list wouldn't be that impressive and you're probably No 1 in at least six categories – I know, I know, 'Only six, you say.' Mr Big Head).

Anyway, Beatriz told her there are a few men missing because she can't remember anything at all about them. Anything! How about that? Even their names. Every now and then a picture will come to her of a certain night – or mid afternoon more likely – and she'll get the briefest image of a hair, or a body, or thigh –she's really into thighs – but no name. Even so, there are over thirty men she *does* remember. All given marks out of five – for sense of humour, smile, how they talk and listen.

Then a column that makes her blush with Alessandra. It's the physical list: orgasm (his/hers, intensity and frequency), body (especially shoulders and thighs), passion, exhaustion, wanting his babies. She calls it her "body-mate" column. The others are under "soul-mate" – if you're going to be locked into eternity you need to joke and laugh a bit. But section two! Alessandra calls it Sextion Two. Beatriz wants her earthly pleasure to be intense (and as frequent as possible). She even subdivides some of the orgasm column. Can his tongue intensify – or delay – her coming? Apparently over two minutes at body-breaking intensity is the record! Then he turns her over and repeats the trick! He should sell tickets.

There's a fantastic bit on how their come tastes. Some are "too salty" – Mr Tonguedemon is rated as "mild". She says it's lovely.

It's all waiting. For news, for work, for my dad to stop saying: "You need to have a plan – he's not coming back, you know." He's always been a planner. Ask mum. He knew where my brother should go to school, who he should marry. I don't think daughters were meant to be part of the deal. Mum always wanted girls. Someone to keep the faith going, someone to talk with instead of listen to. Someone to buy nice dresses with – when we had the money. My brothers have all this religious kit – they even wore it doing the boy stuff – fighting, falling out of trees. "What HAVE you been doing?" must be the question mum asked most when they were small.

We stayed at Joel and Alessandra's house last night. She's made it really beautiful. Flowers everywhere. The smell is wonderful. Then...

Mother sat me down this morning – to talk about love. Her love! Her lover! Get this – NOT father. She's been in love for 30 years, with a dead man.

"Don't let it happen to you Beatriz. Bruno and I met when we were very young – both newly wed – even then we saw it all at once. We would have a lifetime of knowing we had married the wrong person. Our souls would yearn for their soul mate – so near, yet so far. We were lovers for less than a year. But such months we had! Your father spent those days preening himself thinking it was his lust that satisfied me. But it wasn't. It could never be. His lust – do I shock you, Beatriz (Shocked? I was gasping for air) – was only ever tapas before the main feast. Hours of pleasure with Bruno. Sometimes your father's lust was like a strong coffee after a lengthy meal with souls on fire. Then Bruno died – just like that. Cancre. And I kept walking through life with a hole inside. A hole I filled with beautiful children."

Mother bowed her head a little and her cheeks reddened. I saw tears.

"I pray Isidore lives still, my little one."

Now it was my turn. We clutched each other, sobbing. Until Joel marched over with his news: "I'm starting a brewery. With beer from quinua grain." Mother tore me back from this riveting revelation with a whisper – a whisper!

"Falling in love isn't in your control, Beatriz. It's

a wonderfully accurate phrase, isn't it? You fall, with amazing luck, you *both* fall into it. It's like a bottomless, heavenly well. You both tumble, then plunge. Down and down. Holding hands, hearts – whatever comes to hand (a grin – mother really is quite something). I know you know this. But luck never holds you, Beatriz. One day, one of you hits the side of the well. The other keeps falling, always hurting – I almost said hearting. Knowing your souls are no longer bound, no longer one in this life. That somewhere, far above you, lies the broken body that can only be touched now in dreams."

"He sent me a poem more than once. I kept one, it seems to say it all."

Mother looks thoughtful, no more tears and says:

"It's by an Englishman – they must be good for something. Listen.

His heart in me, keeps me and him in one,
My heart in him, his thoughts and senses guides:
He loves my heart for once it was his own:
I cherish his, because in me it bides."

She's right. It says it all. Then she breaks the spell:

"You get to an age when everyone is ill or dying. We lose so many when they are very young. Then, if you make it past having your own children and you manage to avoid hair-brained schemes like the Fortunate Armada, you find yourself surrounded by death. Uncle Valdez, cousin Chaim, both cousins Juan – all dead, none past forty, all taken by the cancre".

And then:

"Let me tell you about ghosts, little one (suddenly I'm ten!). They're everywhere in the house. Ghosts of you and Alessandra playing and laughing. Ghosts of your brother. Small mementoes scattered carefully to remind me wherever I go. I don't know if your father notices. Memory is strange. It lives on in things, not within us, so perhaps he does. He'll see the boat he made your brother when he was about eight and must recall falling in the lake trying to reach out for it.

"But there are ghosts he knows nothing about. That small painting – your father always thought it ugly – but it was given to me by Bruno for my twenty-first birthday. The silk bag in the corner of my room – Bruno's. He made it. The writing desk.

Your father thinks it was my father's, but Bruno made that too. Some of the wine we keep that your father hates. Not Bruno's, but wine we always drank together. Now I drink him with every glass. The tobacco pouch. Mine."

"Yours?"

"Given to me by Bruno when he said it was time I learned how tobacco could take you to a different world."

"Do you still smoke it?"

"Alone, at night. When your father is away."

"Do you still like it?"

Mother pauses:

"Not as much, but it is a world Bruno and I shared so I go there sometimes. I loved that world. And I love him. A dead man brought to life by the memories that live on in small rituals and some precious objects."

That was yesterday. I've read what I wrote and feel, I don't know, sad, a bit lost, but so, so glad to be ALIVE. Is there anything to match just being? I know, I know, 'being with each other' can be pretty good. But, you are gallivanting and I can sit on a beach with memories everywhere. In the sea, the children playing, clouds scudding (a good word, no?). Every moment includes others beaches, other days of sun and laughter. You, me, me as a child, clouds from the past. And on a street, any street – vendors, tapas, sac, children falling into each other.

Try this: a woman walks past looking at her feet. So many women walk like this so other faces and memories flood in – mother going to market, Alessandra going about her business. Or the way she hunches her shoulders. Could be me before you told me about walking upright. What did you say: "Bow your head only before G-d – don't deny others your beauty." WHAT a thing to say. How could a woman walk bowed after that? There are bald men, be-hatted men, adventuros (why are they still here – I think they are looking for other adventures closer to home). A family – two girls, a mother and a father. Is theirs' a happy, family-in-a-box story? Or is the real father long gone, long dead, even on Felipe's mission? And is the man I see here her lover, brother, uncle? They look sunny enough – for once, maybe no tragedy.

A woman is calling us to see the latest offering from a street theatre. One of de la Vega's little gems. "See it now, remember it forever," she cries. But we remember everything forever. It's just that we can't call the memories up by will. They live independently and parade themselves in their own good time. Sometimes good, sometimes bad. Always there for the taking but not the asking.

A rabbi walks past. He has a nerve. And a lovely smile for the children. I'm back in Lugo years ago when mother took care to warn me: "You are a converso. Believe, but lay low. If you see a rabbi, smile for yourself and G-d alone." So I'm smiling. The rabbi sees me and bows a little. Is it *that* obvious? How does he survive the stuffiness at schule on Shabbus? How does he survive at all? There are loads of people now who've taken to calling us 'Marronos' to our faces. Our rabbi treads a very thin line.

Now I see two people dancing in the square. Lovely. And there, in front of me again, are my grandparents – dancers both. They would go wild at bar mitzvahs. I can remember my grandmother dancing on a table. She must have been almost 60.

Truth, you say is love. That's all. But there are so many truths. Sac truth. Bar truth. In-your-cups truth. The truth you tell yourself looking in a mirror – I'm older, younger, prettier, thinner, getting wise with age. Truths when you bet – this is the last time, the penultimate time, the time before the next. I'm a winner, loser, weak. Truth before the first drink of the day – this is a small one, a celebration only, this is too large, I can't stop myself. Truth in bed ('I love you'), truth over breakfast ('Hey, I still love you'). Truth later in the day ('that was fine but I can live without it for a while now').

And now a mystery. Why is it that parents can deal with their female children fucking but not when it's too obvious? I listened to Alessandra yelling for an hour last night and then spent an excruciating hour over breakfast while father went on at her about her lack of discretion. But he knows what she gets up to. Jealousy, maybe. He seems at his most despondent on the way to bed nowadays. Mum always goes to bed first saying she has a headache coming on.

By the way, Alessandra has started listing everything. Dates of birthdays, shopping, which horse father will let her ride that week. She told me she keeps a diary and marks it in stars. 'For what?' I hear you say. Get this. Five stars for a fabulous shag, one for a "let's get it over with duty fuck". She says the scoring is complicated. His orgasms, hers, intensity, frequency, fast, slow, noises (noises!) – she's as bad as the other Beatriz. S'funny she didn't tell me about this list last time we talked about it. Ashamed, maybe?

Alessandra also has a lovely game. Goes like this. You have to list (another list) things about yourself at different ages starting at ten: best friend, where you lived, what you wanted to be when you grew up, where you wanted to live later. Then you do it for 15, 20 and, if you're lucky 25. The game is to see how much changes. It's a bit scary. I don't even remember the name of my best friend at ten. The rest is a bit easier. We've lived in the same house forever, I wanted to be a wife, then your wife and I don't care where I live as long as it's with you. I'll try it with mother.

I'm with my sister and her friend Michaela when Alessandra suddenly says:

"It's a girlie thing."

"What?"

"You know. A woman tries to be straight with her bloke about the state of their relationship. Threatens to leave. Bloke blubs. He's ahead already."

"What brought this on? Problems with Joel? What do you mean, ahead?"

"All a bloke needs to do is blub and he's on the home stretch."

"But he mightn't be doing it deliberately to get that effect. Maybe he's really upset, overwhelmed, whatever. And what on earth has happened?"

"I'm not saying it's deliberate, but neither's my reaction."

"Which is?"

"To feel sorry for him and want him to stop. It's just what we do. Man-child blubs. Woman wants to make it better. So she gives in. Bit like wiping a baby's arse."

"Then what?"

"He goes back to being a miserable, neglectful Pharisee and she spends her time thinking she's a bloody fool and a coward."

"Neglectful? This is new. It's not much of prospect for happiness, is it?"

"Beatriz, it's not about happiness. It's what we do. How many happy couples do you know? I'm not sure I know anybody. People are so good at lying, hiding, whatever."

"You are so cynical?"

"Don't knock it. The cynics lasted 300 years."

What *can* you say to that?

Michaela chimes in: "Thing is, sex is like childbirth."

"What?"

"Well, you know, you forget the details, especially the pain – and you do it over and over."

"Pain?"

"Well, in childbirth obviously you have to go through with it at the time, but you forget it. But pain in sex might put you off. Only might do, though."

"This is getting complicated. Start again."

"What I think is that if you have a fantastic lover, you don't remember the specifics – where he touches, how he touches. You just remember you really liked it and look forward to the next time. Unless there's something odd about it – like his smell or if he's built in a funny way. I think if you go two days without screwing someone then fuck a new man, you won't remember much at all about the first one's breath, body, anything – unless there's been something odd or obnoxious."

"What kind of general things do you remember, then?"

"You know, the fact you've spent all day in bed, just relaxing, eating and screwing. Or, he's clean smelling and always makes you feel loved."

You're clean smelling. You always make me feel loved. I miss you.

"How about the pain?"

"Well, if he's just rough and doesn't care about how I'm reacting, that doesn't do much for me. Or, if he tries to get inside and I'm dry."

"But if you're dry, you don't want him anyway, right?"

"But sometimes pain is just right. Like I love it when Joel pulls my hair."

G-d, I love it when *you* pull my hair. Makes me want to yell: 'Fuck me!'

"Makes me want to yell: 'Fuck me!'"

"What? Are you a mind reader?"

"See, you do know about pain. Isn't it peculiar? Men are obsessed with their cocks but women don't remember cocks in any detail. As long as it's clean and not a funny shape, that's fine," says Michaela. She's growing on me.

"What about the taste?"

"Same. If I'm drunk enough, I don't care about the taste. I give the guy the benefit of the doubt. But if he tastes vile during a sober shag, that's it. Because the other thing kicks in afterwards – the general, 'I don't like this' impression."

I think she's right. I know I love the way you taste and smell but I can't feel it just by thinking about it. The smell thing is worse. Most men don't bother much with perfumes – Bernardo does – so their smells are unique to them. So I can't get reminders of you just by sniffing as I walk through the market. It's not fair.

"It must be really confusing for men, then"

"How?"

"Well, if three lovers wear the same perfume a man will *always* be reminded of another woman, whichever one he's with."

"Don't tell the parfumieres, Beatriz."

In how many different rooms must I think about you? I'm in another now. Mother thought we might stay in town. And what do I think about now I'm here? You. A little drunk, mother keeps looking my way and saying: "What Beatriz?" I'm talking out loud – to you. I just asked if a letter waits at home – that *would* be a wonder.

I think of our room, the mirror (oh G-d, the mirror - and what it might say if only it could speak), the silence all around us in the house – did no-one hear anything at all Mr Screamer?

Here's a love list:

I love trees – forest, woodland, glades, isolated saplings, elderly solitary oaks – you name it. I also love the trees in father's garden. Almost all the trees have been planted and nurtured by him. How about that! As parts have grown wild so clearings have developed that the kids use as dens. All I do is clear the nettles so they can play safer. The garden is no accident. There is order that enables some plants to be seen against particular backgrounds.

I love being in the river with my sister's kids. It's fantastic watching them splashing around or learning to ease their bodies through the water. I am trying to spend more time with them as individuals – reading with Alicia, playing with Miguel on his swing – Dad made it. I've discovered I really enjoy these times. Time feels so precious now.

I have discovered that I love writing. Doesn't make me a writer I know - you once said writers hate writing. But I like the challenge of putting it down, re-reading it. Making it *right*.

Vegetables. Now, there's a thought. I enjoy helping them grow and love cooking them. This is usually bound up with the complexities of family life. Miguel won't eat this and that, Alicia suddenly decides she doesn't want to eat chicken any more. The energy I put into cooking is taken for granted so my carefully thought out combinations of, say, spices and roots are lost on the others – it's all just fuel to them or the backdrop to dinnertime conversation. I suppose this is as it should be. People are happy with the food so can get on with talking to each other – but it's a tired cook who sits down to join in the chat.

I love the stars and the clouds scudding across an expanse of sea. I love the feel of cold salt water and watching the kids racing into the waves.

I didn't want to love any of these things. How can you want to love stars? You just do. But I have learned that so much is saturated with life. And life, my love, I love.

I know too well what it is to lose that which you love and I know also the wisdom of letting go of desire. So I can love all this without fear of loss, only a worry that so much of my energy will have been wasted as the world carries on its merry way laying waste to trees and gardens or introducing those that I love to suffering.

I have survived loss without too much heartache

in the great scheme of things and don't feel an ownership of the life I've helped to maintain. I do appreciate a great deal of what surrounds me and can get overwhelmed with meaning from the past. There are eleven pictures around me as I write. Every one continues to tell a tale – of our home in Lugo, or a holiday near Tui; even the Armada is represented here on father's map. But this is true wherever I am. You can't get to my age without seeing reminders, some sad, some fine, in everything.

I love you. I love Jose. And always shall.

I have the oddest thoughts nowadays. I think it's because I live in a mad world of motherhood, waiting and wanton (am I that wanton?) womanhood and wondering about you, us, the future. This morning, I left Jose asleep in the shade and sat down to sew. And then a thought came. A voice in my head, clear as daylight, asked when I first thought of myself as myself.

For years I have felt ageless (well drifting between eight and thirteen), neither young nor old – but both, all the time. But somewhere there has been an awareness of myself, a kind of looking on at this odd creature while she thinks. While I do that I think about the thoughts and ask: "Who is thinking?" Madder, I wonder who is the "I" thinking about the thinking? How many *mes* are in there? And when did this all start? Was I doing this when Alessandra and I played in the woods as girls? I'm sure I wasn't worried about my skin, being too tall, too thin. Surely, I just played? And what happened to the *I* that was just playing. Is she still in there – here – wherever? The awareness changes things. I write these thoughts down and I'm aware they change. Even time moves on and my pen isn't writing as I think, but a few moments later. The thought must be changed in the time it takes from being part of me to appearing on the page.

So, where did all this begin, where did "Beatriz" start to think of herself as Beatriz - as her thoughts as *her* thoughts? It must have been around the time of my first bleed and mother's urgings for caution and cleanliness. When, suddenly, for a few days each month I was unclean. The punishment for unwed adventures would be a child, the ultimate shame. But having Jose wasn't shameful. It was nothing but joy - well, apart from the agony of his actual birth. There I was with YOUR baby. Our baby. That's it, I became myself when nature forced me to recognise I was an animal and mother pressed on me that I was a woman. A Jewish woman at that. The carrier, the vessel of the faith, no less. No longer a child grazing her knee while climbing trees but a one-day-to-be-mother, wife, lover. I still climb trees though.

At last there's news. People in the streets and markets talk about nothing else. All in whispers. No-one dares talk out loud about "disaster". Recalde has come back, broken they say. He left his ship straightaway to die on dry land in La Corunna. There are so many stories now of dying and starved men. Ships full of the flux and cholera. They say Parma never showed up and Frobisher won battle after battle. The Armada has been blown by gales around the world. What am I meant to believe? One thing for sure – Recalde is back and there's no victory to celebrate.

Sidonia is back too. He needed to be carried from the *San Martin*. There are only ten ships with him. Where are the rest? Where are you? Everyone's got the fever or flux. Apparently all of Sidonia's servants are dead.

This is terrible. Over half the fleet is thought lost. The *Santa Ana* blew up in Santander. How horrible is that? And a hundred poor men went down with her. There are over a thousand sick in port. They won't let them off the ships in case the sickness spreads.

20,000. 20,000! That's how many men are dead. You can't be alive can you? There can be no "us".

There's a new story filling me with fear and hope. I want to believe it's about you, but how can it be? They say a ship arrived at Dongale (?) Bay and anchored at Streedagh (wherever that is). A gale blew up and the ship went down. So many men drowned. So far from home. A hundred? Three? Don Diego Enriquez was drowned and another man sank with the weight of the gold he had sewn into his tunic (how can men do this?). But one was saved, terribly wounded. And stripped by the savages. He was left to die but survived the night and crawled to safety in an abbey. I don't know what they would have made of a nice Jewish boy in an abbey. I know what they made of some of the others. Twelve (some say twenty) stripped and left hanging from the beams. A beautiful girl (this is more like it) took pity on him but stole his asterico davida and hung it round her own neck!

Did you pray? Was it you? He managed to get to a village full of our starving men, then wandered again until an herroro took him in. Father would approve if it was you – "At last! Proper working - with horses", he'd say. Then on to Rosscloja – where do they get these names? Must admit it's the only part of the story I believe so far. No-one could make these town names up. He lived there three months (so that's a few more babies for you) and then he tried his hand at telling people's fortunes.

Well, why not? You were always saying we'd always be together. So you must know the future, smart ass. I think he must have found goodwill amongst the savages – they knew he was fighting the heretics. Or doing his best anyway.

The English marched on Rosscloja – hundreds of them – but our hero agreed to hold the castillo with some of our men while the governor fled. And hold it they did! All ten of them if you can believe it? It must have been quite some castillo. High and moated, no doubt. A trumpeter offered safe conduct to Spain, the siege went on for two weeks, the snow came – and the English gave up! Hmmm...

And now – the only real scene I've witnessed between my parents. The start was bad enough, the finale, horrible. G-d knows what got into mother but she suddenly started talking (quite quietly, over dinner) about marriage. She wondered – in the idlest possible way – if marriages shouldn't be short term agreements rather than for life. She said the "for life" bit was just a combination of romantic nonsense and what suited the powers in charge (Felipe and the church) to guarantee fine young sons, looked after by devoted mothers, to go to war, then die, to keep the people at the top in charge of us all. Then:

"Just shut the fuck up! I swear that I'll hang for that kid if he doesn't stop balling. I need to think. How do you get peace in all this madness?"

"You'll scare him."

"Scare him, I'll bloody throttle him. What are you looking at?"

"My father."

"You're too fucking cheeky for words. Take the kid out before I do something I'll regret."

Mother almost whispers: "Haven't you already?"

"What, marrying you?"

"Showing Beatriz what kind of monster you can be."

"Monster! I'm only yelling. Can you blame me? How can you say all this stuff about having a short-term marriage contract and expect me to be calm?"

"It's not that short term. Three children followed by staying together until the youngest leaves home is usually a long time."

"And then what? You go off with your fancy man?"

"My fancy man is dead!"

"Whaaat?"

All is suddenly silent. They face each other across the table as if they have never seen each other before in their lives. Father's face goes from rage to bemusement to incomprehension, to comprehension and amazement sooner than I can write this. Mother sits quietly waiting for his next words. They don't come. Father stands, turns, glances at me and stalks out.

I'm about to speak to mother who is just starting to sob – and he's back:

"As for you, young woman. You are worse than a whore. You shall marry Bernardo – like it or not."

Sunday

You wouldn't think it possible my parents could argue for forty eight hours. Father was positively ROARING with rage. In the end, I packed Jose's bag and walked to Bernardo's. What a reception – all delighted smiles, even cooing over the baby.

I've been here two days and it really is too unnerving. Here I am in the house of the man I'm supposed to marry and all I think about is you. And what our house would be like. Not as grand as Bernardo's, I can tell you. This place is huge. I've no idea how many bedrooms it has – thirty? I bet Bernardo doesn't know either.

He's made a point of showing me the master bedroom – with the emphasis on master – complete with balcony for having restful, no doubt post-coital, breakfasts. I'm glad I won't be cooking much. There are two kitchens. He sometimes goes down to supervise the cooks but mostly the food just arrives. Like magic. He says he prefers to eat alone when there aren't any guests. I'm not sure what I'm meant to do.

You'd love his study. Filled with books and papers. I caught him this morning deep in thought with a pile of scruffy paper in front of him. He jumped up when I went in and looked – I don't know – guilty? He made a point of putting the papers away before I reached him.

"Bad news?" I asked.

"Nothing to worry about Beatriz. How's Jose?"

If that was his attempt at distraction, it worked.

"Asleep. Getting ready for the big day tomorrow."

Pathetic isn't it? I'm confronted by secrecy and instantly wrong-footed by a question about the boy. Still, he's gone out with some of his cronies tonight so I might get a look at the documents. Probably some investments he doesn't want me to know about. As if I care. Maybe he's broke and scared I won't marry him. He should be – I wouldn't. At least when you decide to marry for money, the contract's clear. And if the money dries up? Adios!

This is fucking incredible. Mother has joined me to "sit quiet for a little" and I've read about half the journal, but she thinks I'm just worried about the wedding. I'm BURSTING. My lord is worse than broke. The papers are YOURS. G-d knows how he got them. He must have been hiding them for ages. Why did he get them out today? Why didn't he burn them? I've been reading for hours. About you, Padraig, Alonzo, dear Wolf. My poor love. How you have suffered. Where in G-d's name *are* you? Are you alive? I don't know what I feel. Up? Down? Empty? Full? Scared? Definitely scared. And I'm furious that he has known that you might be alive for – how long – weeks.

Here I was. All ready to marry him for Jose. Now what? There's no-one to talk to. Least of all you. And I can't bear to give him the chance to lie to me again with some stupid excuse; "I meant to tell you. I forgot. I was going to tell you as soon as we were married."

And if I go through with it? What then? Jose will be safe – known as Jesu from now on. Bernardo's protection for mother and father. Plenty of fine dresses. As many horses as a woman could want. And regret. Can I live with such a sense of what might have been? Sod it! I don't even know if you're alive (how can you be?) and here am I thinking the worst – that you are really out there somewhere while I play happy families. It would be better to know you've drowned (I hope it was quick) or in bed with some English tart so I can think you're happy enough.

Mother is very quiet. She knows how tough this is. But she doesn't know about your diary. It was delicious (too bloody delicious) reading about our sex together. What will sex be like if I marry tomorrow? I won't fake it. I can't. They say some women do but what kind of man doesn't know if his woman is coming? I shall come on demand. I can go somewhere in my head so he'll become you – we, us. I'll yell. He'll be re-assured. I'll be miserable and feel like a whore. And that's what I'll be. But I'm not kidding myself. For the love of Jose and my family, I'll do it.

"You look so sad. You don't have to do this Beatriz."

Can you believe it? Mother's parting words!

Part Three

Coda
Being the decision

I have spoken again with mie lord. He was angrie but saw mie furie and soon calm'd. Yt avail'd hymme nought. He pled for the future of our sonne and said he would rob Jose of hysse inheritance. Yt is I who is disinherited. I have lost two yeares. I thought you drown'd or abandon'd and could hardlie bear yt. Nowe you may still be alive. What am I to do?

I want so much to write – "Mie lord is gone riding. Jose is beside me as I prepare. We leave for Corunna later todaie. I swear bie all that we hold Holy – bie our love and the starres in the night sky – I shall not lose thee again. I shalle search for you. Until death do part us."

I cannot. I shalle marrie. I shalle thank G-d every daie for our love and praie that you are safe. And I shall look to our sonne's future as a mothere must – for love.

By the same author: See also...

Teaching Critical Psychology edited by Newnes and Golding (2018) is available on pre-order from Routledge.

A Critical A to Z of ECT (Newnes, 2018) will be available from Real Press in January 2018.

Clinical Psychology: A critical examination (2014) by Craig Newnes and *Children in Society: Politics, policies and interventions* (2015) edited by Craig Newnes are available from PCCS Books.

For more than you need to know on drugs, ECT and therapy, see: Craig Newnes (2016) *Inscription, Diagnosis, Deception and the Mental Health Industry: How Psy governs us all,* from Palgrave Macmillan.

From the same publisher: See also...

Regicide: Peter Abelard and the Great Jewel, by David Boyle (who killed William Rufus?).

William Shakespeare, Apprentice, by Ursula de Allendesalazar (a fictional version of Shakespeare's lost years as a spy).

www.therealpress.co.uk

Printed in Great Britain
by Amazon